CLASSIC DETECTIVE STORIES

CLASSIC DETECTIVE STORIES
FROM A
SUITCASE OF SUSPENSE

• •

Reader's Digest

The Reader's Digest Association, Inc.
Pleasantville, New York•Montreal

MQ PUBLICATIONS PROJECT STAFF
Project Editor: Nicola Birtwisle
Project Designer: Jason Anscomb

READER'S DIGEST PROJECT STAFF
Project Editor: Nancy Shuker
Project Designer: George McKeon

READER'S DIGEST BOOKS
Editor-in-Chief: Christopher Cavanagh
Executive Editor, Trade Publishing: Dolores York
Senior Design Director: Elizabeth Tunnicliffe
Director, Trade Publishing: Christopher T. Reggio

Library of Congress Cataloging-in-Publication Data

Classic detective stories from a suitcase of suspense.
        p. cm.
     Contents: The adventure of the Sussex vampire / by Arthur Conan Doyle – The blue
geranium / by Agatha Christie – The stolen Rubens / by Jacques Futrelle – Ask me
another / by Frank Gruber – The riddle of the yellow canary / by Stuart Palmer –
Sweating it out with Dover / by Joyce Porter.
     ISBN 0-7621-0371-X
     1. Detective and mystery stories, English. 2. Detective and mystery stories, American.
I. Title: Suitcase of suspense.

PR1309.D4 C555 2002
823'.087208-dc21

                                                                                          2001048632

Address any comments about SUITCASE OF SUSPENSE to:
                The Reader's Digest Association, Inc.
                Adult Trade Publishing
                Reader's Digest Road
                Pleasantville, NY 10570-7000

For more Reader's Digest
products and information,
visit our online store at

rd.com

Printed and bound in China

1 3 5 7 9 10 8 6 4 2

CONTENTS

THE ADVENTURE OF
THE SUSSEX VAMPIRE

BY SIR ARTHUR CONAN DOYLE

Holmes had read carefully a note which the last post had brought him. Then, with the dry chuckle which was his nearest approach to a laugh, he tossed it over to me.

'For a mixture of the modern and the mediaeval, of the practical and of the worldly fanciful, I think this is surely the limit,' said he. 'What do you make of it, Watson?'

I read as follows:

46 OLD JEWRY.
19*th November.*

Re Vampires

SIR,—Our client, Mr Robert Ferguson, of Ferguson and Muirhead, tea brokers, of Mincing Lane, has made some inquiry from us in a communication of even date concerning vampires. As our firm specializes entirely upon the assessment of machinery the matter hardly comes within our purview, and we have therefore recommended Mr Ferguson to call upon you and lay the matter before you. We have not forgotten your successful action in the case of Matilda Briggs.

We are, Sir,

faithfully yours,

MORRISON, MORRISON, AND DODD,
per E.J.C.

'Matilda Briggs was not the name of a young woman, Watson,' said Holmes, in a reminiscent voice. 'It was a ship which is associated with the giant rat of Sumatra, a story for which the world is not yet prepared. But what do we know about vampires? Does it come within our purview either? Anything is better than stagnation, but really we seem to have been switched on to a Grimm's fairy tale. Make a long arm, Watson, and see what V has to say.'

I leaned back and took down the great index volume to which he referred. Holmes balanced it on his knee and his eyes moved slowly and lovingly over the record of old cases, mixed with the accumulated information of a lifetime.

'Voyage of the Gloria Scott,' he read. 'That was a bad business. I have some recollection that you made a record of it, Watson, though I was unable to congratulate you upon the result. Victor Lynch, forger. Venomous lizard or gila. Remarkable case, that! Vittoria, the circus belle. Vanderbilt and the Yeggman. Vipers. Vigor, the Hammersmith wonder. Hullo! Hullo! Good old index. You can't beat it. Listen to this, Watson. Vampirism in Hungary. And again, Vampires in Transylvania.' He turned over the pages with eagerness, but after a short intent perusal he threw down the great book with a snarl of disappointment.

'Rubbish, Watson, rubbish! What have we to do with walking corpses who can only be held in their grave by stakes driven through their hearts? It's pure lunacy.'

'But surely,' said I, 'the vampire was not necessarily a dead man? A living person might have the habit. I have read, for example, of the old sucking the blood of the young in order to retain their youth.'

'You are right, Watson. It mentions the legend in one of these references. But are we to give serious attention to such things? This Agency stands flatfooted upon the ground, and there it must remain. The world is big enough for us. No ghosts need apply. I fear that we cannot take Mr Robert Ferguson very seriously. Possibly this note may be from him, and may throw some light upon what is worrying him.'

He took up a second letter which had lain unnoticed upon the table whilst he had been absorbed with the first. This he began to read with a smile of amusement upon his face which gradually faded away into an expression of intense interest and concentration. When he had finished he sat for some little time lost in thought with the letter dangling from his fingers. Finally, with a start, he aroused himself from his reverie.

'Cheeseman's, Lamberley. Where is Lamberley, Watson?'

'It is in Sussex, south of Horsham.'

'Not very far, eh? And Cheeseman's?'

'I know that country, Holmes. It is full of old houses which are named after the men who built them centuries ago. You get Odley's and Harvey's and Carriton's—the folk are forgotten but their names live in their houses.'

'Precisely,' said Holmes coldly. It was one of the peculiarities of his proud, self-contained nature that, though he docketed any fresh information very quickly and accurately in his brain, he seldom made any acknowledgement to the giver. 'I rather fancy we shall know a good deal more about Cheeseman's, Lamberley, before we are through. The letter is, as I had hoped, from Robert Ferguson. By the way, he claims acquaintance with you.'

'With me!'

'You had better read it.'

He handed the letter across. It was headed with the address quoted.

DEAR MR HOLMES (it said),—I have been recommended to you by my lawyers, but indeed the matter is so extraordinarily delicate that it is most difficult to discuss. It concerns a friend for whom I am acting. This gentleman married some five years ago a Peruvian lady, the daughter of a Peruvian merchant, whom he had met in connection with the importation of nitrates. The lady was very beautiful, but the fact of her foreign birth and of her alien religion always caused a separation of interests and of feelings between husband and wife, so that after a time his love may have cooled towards her and he may have come to regard their union as a mistake. He felt there were sides of her character which he could never explore or understand. This was all the more painful as she was as loving a wife as a man could have —to all appearances absolutely devoted.

Now for the point which I will make more plain when we meet. Indeed, this note is merely to give you a general idea of the situation and to ascertain whether you would care to interest yourself in the matter. The lady began to show some curious traits quite alien to her ordinarily sweet and gentle disposition. The gentleman had been married twice and he had one son by the first wife. This boy was now fifteen, a very charming and affectionate youth, though unhappily injured through an accident in childhood. Twice the wife was caught in the act of assaulting this poor lad in the most unprovoked way. Once she struck him with a stick and left a great weal on his arm.

This was a small matter, however, compared with her conduct to her own child, a dear boy just under one year of age. On one occasion about a month ago this child had been left by its nurse for a few minutes. A loud cry from the baby, as of pain, called the nurse back. As she ran into the room she saw her employer, the lady, leaning over the baby and apparently biting his neck. There was a small wound in the neck, from which a stream of blood had escaped. The nurse was so horrified that she wished to call the husband, but the lady implored her not to do so, and actually gave her five pounds as a price for her silence. No explanation was ever given, and for the moment the matter was passed over.

It left, however, a terrible impression upon the nurse's mind, and from that time she began to watch her mistress closely, and to keep a closer guard upon the baby, whom she tenderly loved. It seemed to her that even as she watched the mother, so the mother watched her, and that every time she was compelled to leave the baby alone the mother was waiting to get at it. Day and night the nurse covered the child, and day and night the silent, watchful mother seemed to be lying in wait as a wolf waits for a lamb. It must read most incredible to you, and yet I beg you to take it seriously, for a child's life and a man's sanity may depend upon it.

At last there came one dreadful day when the facts could no longer be concealed from the husband. The nurse's nerve had given way; she could stand the strain no longer, and she made a clean breast of it all to the man. To him it seemed as wild a tale as it may now seem to you. He knew his wife to be a loving wife, and, save for the assaults upon her stepson, a loving mother. Why, then, should she wound her own dear little boy? He told the nurse that she was dreaming, that her suspicions were those of a lunatic, and that such libels upon her mistress were not to be tolerated. Whilst they were talking, a sudden cry of pain was heard. Nurse and master rushed together to the nursery. Imagine his feelings, Mr Holmes, as he saw his wife rise from a kneeling position beside the cot, and saw blood upon the child's exposed neck and upon the sheet. With a cry of horror, he turned his wife's face to the light and saw blood all round her lips. It was she—beyond all question—who had drunk the poor baby's blood.

So the matter stands. She is now confined to her room. There has been no explanation. The husband is half demented. He knows, and I know, little of Vampirism beyond the name. We had thought it was some wild tale of foreign parts. And yet here in the very heart of the English Sussex—well all this can be discussed with you in the morning. Will you see me? Will you use your great powers in aiding a distracted man? If so, kindly wire to Ferguson, Cheeseman's, Lamberley, and I will be at your rooms by ten o'clock.

Yours faithfully,

ROBERT FERGUSON.

P.S.—I believe your friend Watson played rugby for Blackheath when I was three-quarter for Richmond. It is the only personal introduction which I can give.

'Of course I remember him,' said I, as I laid down the letter. 'Big Bob Ferguson, the finest three-quarter Richmond ever had. He was always a good-natured chap. It's like him to be so concerned over a friend's case.'

Holmes looked at me thoughtfully and shook his head.

'I never get your limits, Watson,' said he. 'There are unexplored possibilities about you. Take a wire down, like a good fellow. "Will examine your case with pleasure."'

'*Your* case!'

'We must not let him think that this Agency is a home for the weak-minded. Of course it is his case. Send him that wire and let the matter rest till morning.'

Promptly at ten o'clock next morning Ferguson strode into our room. I had remembered him as a long, slab-sided man with loose limbs and a fine turn of speed, which had carried him round many an opposing back. There is surely nothing in life more painful than to meet the wreck of a fine athlete whom one has known in his prime. His great frame had fallen in, his flaxen hair was scanty, and his shoulders were bowed. I fear that I roused corresponding emotions in him.

'Hullo, Watson,' said he, and his voice was still deep and hearty. 'You don't look quite the man you did when I threw you over the ropes into the crowd at the Old Deer Park. I expect I have changed a bit also. But it's this last day or two that has aged me. I see by your telegram, Mr Holmes, that it is no use my pretending to be anyone's deputy.'

'It is simpler to deal direct,' said Holmes.

'Of course it is. But you can imagine how difficult it is when you are speaking of the one woman you are bound to protect and help. What can I do? How am I to go to the police with such a story? And yet the kiddies have got to be protected. Is it madness, Mr Holmes? Is it something in the blood? Have you any similar case in your experience? For God's sake, give me some advice, for I am at my wits' end.'

'Very naturally, Mr Ferguson. Now sit here and pull yourself together and give me a few clear answers. I can assure you that I am very far from being at my wits' end, and that I am confident we shall find some solution. First of all, tell me what steps you have taken. Is your wife still near the children?'

'We had a dreadful scene. She is a most loving woman, Mr Holmes. If ever a woman loved a man with all her heart and soul, she loves me. She was cut to the heart that I should have discovered this horrible, this incredible, secret. She would not even speak. She gave no answer to my reproaches, save to gaze at me with a sort of wild, despairing look in her eyes. Then she rushed to her room and locked herself in. Since then she has refused to see me. She has a maid who was with her before her marriage, Dolores by name—a friend rather than a servant. She takes her food to her.'

'Then the child is in no immediate danger?'

'Mrs Mason, the nurse, has sworn that she will not leave it night or day. I can absolutely trust her. I am more uneasy about poor little Jack, for, as I told you in my note, he has twice been assaulted by her.'

'But never wounded?'

'No; she struck him savagely. It is the more terrible as he is a poor little inoffensive cripple.' Ferguson's gaunt features softened as he spoke of his boy. 'You would think that the dear lad's condition would soften anyone's heart. A fall in childhood and a twisted spine, Mr Holmes. But the dearest, most loving heart within.'

Holmes had picked up the letter of yesterday and was reading it over. 'What other inmates are there in your house, Mr Ferguson?'

'Two servants who have not been long with us. One stablehand, Michael, who sleeps in the house. My wife, myself, my boy Jack, baby, Dolores, and Mrs Mason. That is all.'

'I gather that you did not know your wife well at the time of your marriage?'

'I had only known her a few weeks.'

'How long had this maid Dolores been with her?'

'Some years.'

'Then your wife's character would really be better known by Dolores than by you?'

'Yes, you may say so.'

Holmes made a note.

'I fancy,' said he, 'that I may be of more use at Lamberley than here. It is eminently a case for personal investigation. If the lady remains in her room, our presence could not annoy or inconvenience her. Of course, we would stay at the inn.'

Ferguson gave a gesture of relief.

'It is what I hoped, Mr Holmes. There is an excellent train at two from Victoria, if you could come.'

'Of course we could come. There is a lull at present. I can give you my undivided energies. Watson, of course, comes with us. But there are one or two points upon which I wish to be very sure before I start. This unhappy lady, as I understand it, has appeared to assault both the children, her own baby and your little son?'

'That is so.'

'But the results take different forms, do they not? She has beaten your son.'

'Once with a stick and once very savagely with her hands.'

'Did she give no explanation why she struck him?'

'None, save that she hated him. Again and again she said so.'

'Well, that is not unknown among stepmothers. A posthu-mous jealousy, we will say. Is the lady jealous by nature?'

'Yes, she is very jealous—jealous with all the strength of her fiery tropical love.'

'But the boy—he is fifteen, I understand, and probably very developed in mind, since his body has been circumscribed in action. Did he give you no explanation of these assaults?'

'No; he declared there was no reason.'

'Were they good friends at other times?'

'No; there was never any love between them.'

'Yet you say he is affectionate?'

'Never in the world could there be so devoted a son. My life is his life. He is absorbed in what I say or do.'

Once again Holmes made a note. For some time he sat lost in thought.

'No doubt you and the boy were very great comrades before this second marriage. You were thrown very close together, were you not?'

'Very much so.'

'And the boy, having so affectionate a nature, was devoted, no doubt, to the memory of his mother?'

'Most devoted.'

'He would certainly seem to be a most interesting lad. There is one other point about these assaults. Were the strange attacks upon the baby and the assaults upon your son at the same period?'

'In the first case it was so. It was as if some frenzy had seized her, and she had vented her rage upon both. In the second case it was only Jack who suffered. Mrs Mason had no complaint to make about the baby.'

'That certainly complicates matters.'

'I don't quite follow you, Mr Holmes.'

'Possibly not. One forms provisional theories and waits for time or fuller knowledge to explode them. A bad habit, Mr Ferguson; but human nature is weak. I fear that your old friend here has given an exaggerated view of my scientific methods. However, I will only say at the present stage that your problem does not appear to me to be insoluble, and that you may expect to find us at Victoria at two o'clock.'

It was evening of a dull, foggy November day when, having left our bags at the 'Chequers', Lamberley, we drove through the Sussex clay of a long winding lane, and finally reached the isolated and ancient farm-house in which Ferguson dwelt. It was a large, straggling building, very old in the centre, very new at the wings, with towering Tudor chimneys and a lichen-spotted, high-pitched roof of Horsham slabs. The doorsteps were worn into curves, and the ancient tiles which lined the porch were marked with the rebus of a cheese and a man, after the original builder. Within, the ceilings were corrugated with heavy oaken beams, and the uneven floors sagged into sharp curves. An odour of age and decay pervaded the whole crumbling building.

There was one very large central room, into which Ferguson led us. Here, in a huge old-fashioned fireplace with an iron screen behind it dated 1670, there blazed and spluttered a splendid log fire.

The room, as I gazed round, was a most singular mixture

of dates and of places. The half-panelled walls may well have belonged to the original yeoman farmer of the seventeenth century. They were ornamented, however, on the lower part by a line of well-chosen modern water-colours; while above, where yellow plaster took the place of oak, there was hung a fine collection of South American utensils and weapons, which had been brought, no doubt, by the Peruvian lady upstairs. Holmes rose, with that quick curiosity which sprang from his eager mind, and examined them with some care. He returned with eyes full of thought.

'Hullo!' he cried. 'Hullo!'

A spaniel had lain in a basket in the corner. It came slowly forward towards its master, walking with difficulty. Its hind-legs moved irregularly and its tail was on the ground. It licked Ferguson's hand.

'What is it, Mr Holmes?'

'The dog. What's the matter with it?'

'That's what puzzled the vet. A sort of paralysis. Spinal meningitis, he thought. But it is passing. He'll be all right soon—won't you, Carlo?'

A shiver of assent passed through the drooping tail. The dog's mournful eyes passed from one of us to the other. He knew that we were discussing his case.

'Did it come on suddenly?'

'In a single night.'

'How long ago?'

'It may have been four months ago.'

'Very remarkable. Very suggestive.'

'What do you see in it, Mr Holmes?'

'A confirmation of what I had already thought.'

'For God's sake, what *do* you think, Mr Holmes? It may be a mere intellectual puzzle to you, but it is life and death to me! My wife a would-be murderer—my child in constant danger! Don't play with me, Mr Holmes. It is too terribly serious.'

The big rugby three-quarter was trembling all over. Holmes put his hand soothingly upon his arm.

'I fear that there is pain for you, Mr Ferguson, whatever the solution may be,' said he. 'I would spare you all I can. I cannot say more for the instant, but before I leave this house I hope I may have something definite.'

'Please God you may! If you will excuse me, gentlemen, I will go up to my wife's room and see if there has been any change.'

He was away some minutes, during which Holmes resumed his examination of the curiosities upon the wall. When our host returned it was clear from his downcast face that he had made no progress. He brought with him a tall, slim, brown-faced girl.

'The tea is ready, Dolores,' said Ferguson. 'See that your mistress has everything she can wish.'

'She verra ill,' cried the girl, looking with indignant eyes at her master. 'She no ask for food. She verra ill. She need doctor. I frightened stay alone with her without doctor.'

Ferguson looked at me with a question in his eyes.

'I should be so glad if I could be of use.'

'Would your mistress see Dr Watson?'

'I take him. I no ask leave. She needs doctor.'

'Then I'll come with you at once.'

I followed the girl, who was quivering with strong emotion, up the staircase and down an ancient corridor. At the end was an iron-clamped and massive door. It struck me as I looked at it that if Ferguson tried to force his way to his wife he would find it no easy matter. The girl drew a key from her pocket, and the heavy oaken planks creaked upon their old hinges. I passed in and she swiftly followed, fastening the door behind her.

On the bed a woman was lying who was clearly in a high fever. She was only half conscious, but as I entered she raised a pair of frightened but beautiful eyes and glared at me in apprehension. Seeing a stranger, she appeared to be relieved, and sank back with a sigh upon the pillow. I stepped up to her with a few reassuring words, and she lay still while I took her pulse and temperature. Both were high, and yet my impression was that the condition was rather that of mental and nervous excitement than of any actual seizure.

'She lie like that one day, two day. I 'fraid she die,' said the girl.

The woman turned her flushed and handsome face towards me.

'Where is my husband?'

'He is below, and would wish to see you.'

'I will not see him. I will not see him.' Then she seemed to wander off into delirium. 'A fiend! A fiend! Oh, what shall I do with this devil?'

'Can I help you in any way?'

'No. No one can help. It is finished. All is destroyed. Do what I will, all is destroyed.'

21

The woman must have some strange delusion. I could not see honest Bob Ferguson in the character of fiend or devil.

'Madame,' I said, 'your husband loves you dearly. He is deeply grieved at this happening.'

Again she turned on me those glorious eyes.

'He loves me. Yes. But do I not love him? Do I not love him even to sacrifice myself rather than break his dear heart. That is how I love him. And yet he could think of me—he could speak to me so.'

'He is full of grief, but he cannot understand.'

'No, he cannot understand. But he should trust.'

'Will you not see him?' I suggested.

'No, no; I cannot forget those terrible words nor the look upon his face. I will not see him. Go now. You can do nothing for me. Tell him only one thing. I want my child. I have a right to my child. That is the only message I can send him.' She turned her face to the wall and would say no more.

I returned to the room downstairs, where Ferguson and Holmes still sat by the fire. Ferguson listened moodily to my account of the interview.

'How can I send her the child?' he said. 'How do I know what strange impulse might come upon her? How can I ever forget how she rose from beside it with its blood on her lips?' He shuddered at the recollection. 'This child is safe with Mrs Mason, and there he must remain.'

A smart maid, the only modern thing which we had seen in the house, had brought in some tea. As she was serving it the door opened and a youth entered the room. He was a remarkable lad, pale-faced and fair-haired, with excitable light blue eyes which blazed into a sudden flame of emotion and joy as they rested upon his father. He rushed forward and threw his arms round his neck with the abandon of a loving girl.

'Oh, daddy,' he cried, 'I did not know that you were due yet. I should have been here to meet you. Oh, I am so glad to see you!'

Ferguson gently disengaged himself from the embrace with some little show of embarrassment.

'Dear old chap,' said he, patting the flaxen head with a very tender hand. 'I came early because my friends, Mr Holmes and Dr Watson, have been persuaded to come down and spend an evening with us.'

'Is that Mr Holmes, the detective?'

'Yes.'

The youth looked at us with a very penetrating and, as it seemed to me, unfriendly gaze.

'What about your other child, Mr Ferguson?' asked Holmes. 'Might we make the acquaintance of the baby?'

'Ask Mrs Mason to bring baby down,' said Ferguson.

The boy went off with a curious, shambling gait which told my surgical eyes that he was suffering from a weak spine. Presently he returned, and behind him came a tall, gaunt woman bearing in her arms a very beautiful child, golden-haired, a wonderful mixture of the Saxon and the Latin. Ferguson was evidently devoted to it, for he took it into his arms and fondled it most tenderly.

'Fancy anyone having the heart to hurt him,' he muttered,

as he glanced down at the small, angry red pucker upon the cherub throat.

It was at this moment that I chanced to glance at Holmes and saw a most singular intentness in his expression. His face was as set as if it had been carved out of old ivory, and his eyes, which had glanced for a moment at father and child, were now fixed with eager curiosity upon something at the other side of the room. Following his gaze I could only guess that he was looking out through the window at the melancholy, dripping garden. It is true that a shutter had half closed outside and obstructed the view, but none the less it was certainly at the window that Holmes was fixing his concentrated attention. Then he smiled, and his eyes came back to the baby. On its chubby neck there was this small puckered mark. Without speaking, Holmes examined it with care. Finally he shook one of the dimpled fists which waved in front of him.

'Good-bye, little man. You have made a strange start in life. Nurse, I should wish to have a word with you in private.'

He took her aside and spoke earnestly for a few minutes. I only heard the last words, which were: 'Your anxiety will soon, I hope, be set at rest.' The woman, who seemed to be a sour, silent kind of creature, withdrew with the child.

'What is Mrs Mason like?' asked Holmes.

'Not very prepossessing externally, as you can see, but a heart of gold, and devoted to the child.'

'Do you like her, Jack?' Holmes turned suddenly upon the boy. His expressive, mobile face shadowed over, and he shook his head.

'Jacky has very strong likes and dislikes,' said Ferguson, putting his arm round the boy. 'Luckily I am one of his likes.'

The boy cooed and nestled his head upon his father's breast. Ferguson gently disengaged him.

'Run away, little Jacky,' said he, and he watched his son with loving eyes until he disappeared. 'Now, Mr Holmes,' he continued, when the boy was gone, 'I really feel that I have brought you on a fool's errand, for what can you possibly do, save give your sympathy? It must be an exceedingly delicate and complex affair from your point of view.'

'It is certainly delicate,' said my friend, with an amused smile, 'but I have not been struck up to now with its complexity. It has been a case for intellectual deduction, but when this original intellectual deduction is confirmed point by point by quite a number of independent incidents, then the subjective becomes objective and we can say confidently that we have reached our goal. I had, in fact, reached it before we left Baker Street, and the rest has merely been observation and confirmation.'

Ferguson put his big hand to his furrowed forehead.

'For Heaven's sake, Holmes,' he said hoarsely, 'if you can see the truth in this matter, do not keep me in suspense. How do I stand? What shall I do? I care nothing as to how you have found your facts so long as you have really got them.'

'Certainly I owe you an explanation, and you shall have it. But you will permit me to handle the matter in my own way? Is the lady capable of seeing us, Watson?'

'She is ill, but she is quite rational.'

'Very good. It is only in her presence that we can clear the matter up. Let us go up to her.'

'She will not see me,' cried Ferguson.

'Oh, yes, she will,' said Holmes. He scribbled a few lines upon a sheet of paper. 'You at least have the entrée, Watson. Will you have the goodness to give the lady this note?'

I ascended again and handed the note to Dolores, who cautiously opened the door. A minute later I heard a cry from within, a cry in which joy and surprise seemed to be blended. Dolores looked out.

'She will see them. She will leesten,' said she.

At my summons Ferguson and Holmes came up. As we entered the room Ferguson took a step or two towards his wife, who had raised herself in the bed, but she held out her hand to repulse him. He sank into an arm-chair, while Holmes seated himself beside him, after bowing to the lady, who looked at him with wide-eyed amazement.

'I think we can dispense with Dolores,' said Holmes. 'Oh, very well, madame, if you would rather she stayed I can see no objection. Now, Mr Ferguson, I am a busy man with many calls, and my methods have to be short and direct. The swiftest surgery is the least painful. Let me first say what will ease your mind. Your wife is a very good, a very loving, and a very ill-used woman.'

Ferguson sat up with a cry of joy.

'Prove that, Mr Holmes, and I am your debtor for ever.'

'I will do so, but in doing so I must wound you deeply in another direction.'

'I care nothing so long as you clear my wife. Everything on earth is insignificant compared to that.'

'Let me tell you, then, the train of reasoning which passed though my mind in Baker Street. The idea of a vampire was to me absurd. Such things do not happen in criminal practice in England. And yet your observation was precise. You had seen the lady rise from beside the child's cot with the blood upon her lips.'

'I did.'

'Did it not occur to you that a bleeding wound may be sucked for some other purpose than to draw the blood from it? Was there not a Queen in English history who sucked such a wound to draw poison from it?'

'Poison!'

'A South American household. My instinct felt the presence of those weapons upon the wall before my eyes ever saw them. It might have been other poison, but that was what occurred to me. When I saw that little empty quiver beside the small bird-bow, it was just what I expected to see. If the child were pricked with one of those arrows dipped in curare or some other devilish drug, it would mean death if the venom were not sucked out.

'And the dog! If one were to use such a poison, would one not try it first in order to see that it had not lost its power? I did not foresee the dog, but at least I understand him and he fitted into my reconstruction.

'Now do you understand? Your wife feared such an attack. She saw it made and saved the child's life, and yet she shrank from telling you all the truth, for she knew how you loved the boy and feared lest it break your heart.'

'Jacky!'

'I watched him as you fondled the child just now. His face was clearly reflected in the glass of the window where the shutter formed a background. I saw such jealousy, such cruel hatred, as I have seldom seen in a human face.'

'My Jacky!'

'You have to face it, Mr Ferguson. It is the more painful because it is distorted love, a maniacal exaggerated love for you, and possibly for his dead mother, which has prompted his action. His very soul is consumed with hatred for this splendid child, whose health and beauty are a contrast to his own weakness.'

'Good God! It is incredible!'

'Have I spoken the truth, madame?'

The lady was sobbing, with her face buried in the pillows. Now she turned to her husband.

'How could I tell you, Bob? I felt the blow it would be to you. It was better that I should wait and that it should come from some other lips than mine. When this gentleman, who seems to have powers of magic, wrote that he knew all, I was glad.'

'I think a year at sea would be my prescription for Master Jacky,' said Holmes, rising from his chair. 'Only one thing is still clouded, madame. We can quite understand your attacks upon Master Jacky. There is a limit to a mother's patience. But how did you dare to leave the child these last two days?'

'I had told Mrs Mason. She knew.'

'Exactly. So I imagined.'

Ferguson was standing by the bed, choking, his hands outstretched and quivering.

'This, I fancy, is the time for our exit, Watson,' said Holmes in a whisper. 'If you will take one elbow of the too faithful Dolores, I will take the other. There, now,' he added, as he closed the door behind him, 'I think we may leave them to settle the rest among themselves.'

I have only one further note in this case. It is the letter which Holmes wrote in final answer to that with which the narrative begins. It ran thus:

BAKER STREET
21st November

Re Vampires

SIR,—Referring to your letter of the 19th, I beg to state that I have looked into the inquiry of your client, Mr Robert Ferguson, of Ferguson and Muirhead, tea brokers, of Mincing Lane, and that the matter has been brought to a satisfactory conclusion. With thanks for your recommendation,

I am, Sir,
Faithfully yours,
SHERLOCK HOLMES.

THE BLUE GERANIUM

BY AGATHA CHRISTIE

'When I was down here last year—' said Sir Henry Clithering, and stopped.

His hostess, Mrs Bantry, looked at him curiously.

The Ex-Commissioner of Scotland Yard was staying with old friends of his, Colonel and Mrs Bantry, who lived near St Mary Mead.

Mrs Bantry, pen in hand, had just asked his advice as to who should be invited to make a sixth guest at dinner that evening.

'Yes?' said Mrs Bantry, encouragingly. 'When you were here last year?'

'Tell me,' said Sir Henry, 'do you know a Miss Marple?'

Mrs Bantry was surprised. It was the last thing she had expected.

'Know Miss Marple? Who doesn't? The typical old maid of fiction. Quite a dear, but hopelessly behind the times. Do you mean you would like me to ask *her* to dinner?'

'You are surprised?'

'A little, I must confess. I should hardly have thought you —but perhaps there's an explanation?'

'The explanation is simple enough. When I was down here last year we got into the habit of discussing unsolved mysteries—there were five or six of us—Raymond West, the novelist, started it. We each supplied a story to which we knew the answer, but nobody else did. It was supposed to be an exercise in the deductive faculties—to see who could get nearest the truth.'

'Well?'

'Like in the old story—we hardly realized that Miss Marple was playing; but we were very polite about it—didn't want to hurt the old dear's feelings. And now comes the cream of the jest. The old lady outdid us every time!'

'What?'

'I assure you—straight to the truth like a homing pigeon.'

'But how extraordinary! Why, dear old Miss Marple has hardly ever been out of St Mary Mead.'

'Ah! But according to her, that has given her unlimited opportunities of observing human nature—under the microscope as it were.'

'I suppose there's something in that,' conceded Mrs Bantry. 'One would at least know the petty side of people. But I don't think we have any really exciting criminals in our midst. I think we must try her with Arthur's ghost story after dinner. I'd be thankful if she'd find a solution to that.'

'I didn't know that Arthur believed in ghosts?'

'Oh! he doesn't. That's what worries him so. And it happened to a friend of his, George Pritchard—a most prosaic person. It's really rather tragic for poor George. Either this extraordinary story is true—or else—'

'Or else what?'

Mrs Bantry did not answer. After a minute or two she said irrelevantly:

'You know, I like George—everyone does. One can't believe that he—but people do do such extraordinary things.'

Sir Henry nodded. He knew, better than Mrs Bantry, the extraordinary things that people did.

So it came about that that evening Mrs Bantry looked round her dinner table (shivering a little as she did so, because the dining-room, like most English dining-rooms, was extremely cold) and fixed her gaze on the very upright old lady sitting on her husband's right. Miss Marple wore black lace mittens; an old lace fichu was draped round her shoulders and another piece of lace surmounted her white hair. She was talking animatedly to the elderly doctor, Dr Lloyd, about the Workhouse and the suspected shortcomings of the District Nurse.

Mrs Bantry marvelled anew. She even wondered whether Sir Henry had been making an elaborate joke—but there seemed no point in that. Incredible that what he had said could be really true.

Her glance went on and rested affectionately on her red-faced, broad-shouldered husband as he sat talking horses to Jane Helier, the beautiful and popular actress. Jane, more beautiful (if that were possible) off the stage than on, opened enormous blue eyes and murmured at discreet intervals: 'Really?' 'Oh fancy!' 'How extraordinary!' She knew nothing whatever about horses and cared less.

'Arthur,' said Mrs Bantry, 'you're boring poor Jane to distraction. Leave horses alone and tell her your ghost story instead. You know…George Pritchard.'

'Eh, Dolly? Oh! but I don't know—'

'Sir Henry wants to hear it too. I was telling him something about it this morning. It would be interesting to hear what everyone has to say about it.'

'Oh, do!' said Jane. 'I love ghost stories.'

'Well—' Colonel Bantry hesitated. 'I've never believed much in the supernatural. But this—

'I don't think any of you know George Pritchard. He's one of the best. His wife—well, she's dead now, poor woman. I'll just say this much: she didn't give George any too easy a time when she was alive. She was one of those semi-invalids—I believe she had really something wrong with her, but whatever it was she played it for all it was worth. She was capricious, exacting, unreasonable. She complained from morning to night. George was expected to wait on her hand and foot, and everything he did was always wrong and he got cursed for it. Most men, I'm fully convinced, would have hit her over the head with a hatchet long ago. Eh, Dolly, isn't that so?'

'She was a dreadful woman,' said Mrs Bantry with conviction. 'If George Pritchard had brained her with a hatchet, and there had been any woman on the jury, he would have been triumphantly acquitted.'

'I don't quite know how this business started. George was rather vague about it. I gather Mrs Pritchard had always had a weakness for fortune-tellers, palmists, clairvoyantes—anything of that sort. George didn't mind. If she found amusement in it, well and good. But he refused to go into rhapsodies himself, and that was another grievance.

'A succession of hospital nurses was always passing through the house, Mrs Pritchard usually becoming dissatisfied with them after a few weeks. One young nurse had been very keen on this fortune-telling stunt, and for a time Mrs Pritchard had been very fond of her. Then she suddenly fell out with her and insisted on her going. She had back another nurse who had been with her previously—an older woman, experienced and tactful in dealing with a neurotic patient. Nurse Copling, according to George, was a very good sort—a sensible woman to talk to. She put up with Mrs Pritchard's tantrums and nerve-storms with complete indifference.

'Mrs Pritchard always lunched upstairs, and it was usual at lunch time for George and the nurse to come to some arrangement for the afternoon. Strictly speaking, the nurse went off from two to four, but "to oblige," as the phrase goes, she would sometimes take her time off after tea if George wanted to be free for the afternoon. On this occasion, she mentioned that she was going to see a sister at Golders Green and might be a little late returning. George's face fell, for he had arranged to play a round of golf. Nurse Copling, however, reassured him.

' "We'll neither of us be missed, Mr Pritchard." A twinkle came into her eye. "Mrs Pritchard's going to have more exciting company than ours."

' "Who's that?"

' "Wait a minute," Nurse Copling's eyes twinkled more than ever. "Let me get it right. *Zarida, Psychic Reader of the Future.*"

' "Oh Lord!" groaned George. "That's a new one, isn't it?"

' "Quite new. I believe my predecessor, Nurse Carstairs, sent her along. Mrs Pritchard hasn't seen her yet. She made me write, fixing an appointment for this afternoon."

' "Well, at any rate, I shall get my golf," said George, and he went off with the kindliest feelings towards Zarida, the Reader of the Future.

'On his return to the house, George found Mrs Pritchard in a state of great agitation. She was, as usual, lying on her invalid couch, and she had a bottle of smelling-salts in her hand which she sniffed at frequent intervals.

' "George," she exclaimed. "What did I tell you about this house? The moment I came into it, I *felt* there was something wrong! Didn't I tell you so at the time?"

'Repressing his desire to reply, "You always do," George said, "No, I can't say I remember it."

' "You never do remember anything that has to do with me. Men are all extraordinarily callous—but I really believe that you are even more insensitive than most."

' "Oh, come now, Mary dear, that's not fair."

' "Well, as I was telling you, this woman *knew* at once! She —she actually blenched—if you know what I mean—as she came in at that door, and she said: 'There is evil here—evil and danger. I feel it.' "

'Very unwisely George laughed.

' "Well, you have had your money's worth this afternoon."

'His wife closed her eyes and took a long sniff from her smelling bottle.

' "How you hate me! You would jeer and laugh if I were dying."

'George protested, and after a minute or two she went on.

' "You may laugh, but I shall tell you the whole thing. This house is definitely dangerous to me—the woman said so."

'George's formerly kind feeling towards Zarida underwent a change. He knew his wife was perfectly capable of insisting on moving to a new house if the caprice got hold of her.

' "What else did she say?" he asked.

' "She couldn't tell me very much. She was so upset. One thing she did say. I had some violets in a glass. She pointed at them and cried out:

' " 'Take those away. No blue flowers—never have blue flowers. *Blue flowers are fatal to you—remember that.*' "

' "And you know," added Mrs Pritchard, "I always have told you that blue as a colour is repellent to me. I feel a natural instinctive sort of warning against it."

'George was much too wise to remark that he had never heard her say so before. Instead he asked what the mysterious Zarida was like. Mrs Pritchard entered with gusto upon a description.

' "Black hair in coiled knobs over her ears—her eyes were half-closed—great black rims round them—she had a black veil over her mouth and chin—and she spoke in a kind of singing voice with a marked foreign accent—Spanish, I think—"

' "In fact all the usual stock-in-trade," said George cheerfully.

'His wife immediately closed her eyes.

' "I feel extremely ill," she said. "Ring for nurse. Unkindness upsets me, as you know only too well."

'It was two days later that Nurse Copling came to George with a grave face.

' "Will you come to Mrs Pritchard, please? She has had a letter which upsets her greatly."

'He found his wife with the letter in her hand. She held it out to him.

' "Read it," she said.

'George read it. It was on heavily scented paper, and the writing was big and black.

'*I have seen the future. Be warned before it is too late. Beware of the Full Moon. The Blue Primrose means Warning; the Blue Hollyhock means Danger; the Blue Geranium means Death...*

'Just about to burst out laughing, George caught Nurse Copling's eye. She made a quick warning gesture. He said rather awkwardly, "The woman's probably trying to frighten you, Mary. Anyway there aren't such things as blue primroses and blue geraniums."

'But Mrs Pritchard began to cry and say her days were numbered. Nurse Copling came out with George upon the landing.

' "Of all the silly tomfoolery," he burst out.

' "I suppose it is."

'Something in the nurse's tone struck him, and he stared at her in amazement.

' "Surely, nurse, you don't believe—"

' "No, no, Mr Pritchard. I don't believe in reading the future—that's nonsense. What puzzles me is the *meaning* of this. Fortune-tellers are usually out for what they can get. But this woman seems to be frightening Mrs Pritchard with no advantage to herself. I can't see the point. There's another thing—"

' "Yes?"

' "Mrs Pritchard says that something about Zarida was faintly familiar to her."

' "Well?"

' "Well, I don't like it, Mr Pritchard, that's all."

' "I didn't know you were so superstitious, nurse."

' "I'm not superstitious; but I know when a thing is fishy."

'It was about four days after this that the first incident happened. To explain it to you, I shall have to describe Mrs Pritchard's room—'

'You'd better let me do that,' interrupted Mrs Bantry. 'It was papered with one of these new wallpapers where you apply clumps of flowers to make a kind of herbaceous border. The effect is almost like being in a garden—though, of course, the flowers are all wrong. I mean they simply couldn't be in bloom all at the same time—'

'Don't let a passion for horticultural accuracy run away

with you, Dolly,' said her husband. 'We all know you're an enthusiastic gardener.'

'Well, it *is* absurd,' protested Mrs Bantry. 'To have bluebells and daffodils and lupins and hollyhocks and Michaelmas daisies all grouped together.'

'Most unscientific,' said Sir Henry. 'But to proceed with the story.'

'Well, among these massed flowers were primroses, clumps of yellow and pink primroses and—oh go on, Arthur, this is your story—'

Colonel Bantry took up the tale.

'Mrs Pritchard rang her bell violently one morning. The household came running—thought she was in extremis; not at all. She was violently excited and pointing at the wallpaper; and there sure enough was *one blue primrose* in the midst of the others...'

'Oh!' said Miss Helier, 'how creepy!'

'The question was: Hadn't the blue primrose always been there? That was George's suggestion and the nurse's. But Mrs Pritchard wouldn't have it at any price. She had never noticed it till that very morning, and the night before had been full moon. She was very upset about it.'

'I met George Pritchard that same day and he told me about it,' said Mrs Bantry. 'I went to see Mrs Pritchard and did my best to ridicule the whole thing; but without success. I came away really concerned, and I remember I met Jean Instow and told her about it. Jean is a queer girl. She said, "So she's really upset about it?" I told her that I thought the woman was perfectly capable of dying of fright—she was really abnormally superstitious.

'I remember Jean rather startled me with what she said next. She said, "Well, that might be all for the best, mightn't it?" And she said it so coolly, in so matter-of-fact a tone that I was really—well, shocked. Of course I know it's done nowadays—to be brutal and outspoken; but I never get used to it. Jean smiled at me rather oddly and said, "You don't like my saying that—but it's true. What use is Mrs Pritchard's life to her? None at all; and it's hell for George Pritchard. To have his wife frightened out of existence would be the best thing that could happen to him." I said, "George is most awfully good to her always." And she said, "Yes, he deserves a reward, poor dear. He's a very attractive person, George Pritchard. The last nurse thought so—the pretty one—what was her name? Carstairs. That was the cause of the row between her and Mrs P."

'Now I didn't like hearing Jean say that. Of course one had *wondered*—'

Mrs Bantry paused significantly.

'Yes, dear,' said Miss Marple placidly. 'One always does. Is Miss Instow a pretty girl? I suppose she plays golf?'

'Yes. She's good at all games. And she's nice looking, attractive-looking, very fair with a healthy skin, and nice steady blue eyes. Of course we always have felt that she and George Pritchard—I mean if things had been different—they are so well suited to one another.'

'And they were friends?' asked Miss Marple.

'Oh yes. Great friends.'

'Do you think, Dolly,' said Colonel Bantry plaintively, 'that I might be allowed to go on with my story?'

'Arthur,' said Mrs Bantry resignedly, 'wants to get back to his ghosts.'

'I had the rest of the story from George himself,' went on the colonel. 'There's no doubt that Mrs Pritchard got the wind up badly towards the end of the next month. She marked off on a calendar the day when the moon would be full, and on that night she had both the nurse and then George into her room and made them study the wallpaper carefully. There were pink hollyhocks and red ones, but there were no blue amongst them. Then when George left the room she locked the door—'

'And in the morning there was a large blue hollyhock,' said Miss Helier joyfully.

'Quite right,' said Colonel Bantry. 'Or at any rate, nearly right. One flower of a hollyhock just above her head had turned blue. It staggered George; and of course the more it staggered him the more he refused to take the thing seriously. He insisted that the whole thing was some kind of practical joke. He ignored the evidence of the locked door and the fact that Mrs Pritchard discovered the change before anyone—even Nurse Copling—was admitted.

'It staggered George; and it made him unreasonable. His wife wanted to leave the house, and he wouldn't let her. He was inclined to believe in the supernatural for the first time, but he wasn't going to admit it. He usually gave in to his wife, but this time he wouldn't. Mary was not to make a fool of herself, he said. The whole thing was the most infernal nonsense.

'And so the next month sped away. Mrs Pritchard made less protest than one would have imagined. I think she was superstitious enough to believe that she couldn't escape her fate. She repeated again and again: "The blue primrose—warning. The blue hollyhock—danger. The blue geranium—*death*." And she would lie looking at the clump of pinky-red geraniums nearest her bed.

'The whole business was pretty nervy. Even the nurse caught the infection. She came to George two days before full moon and begged him to take Mrs Pritchard away. George was angry.

' "If all the flowers on that damned wall turned into blue devils it couldn't kill anyone!" he shouted.

' "It might. Shock has killed people before now."

' "Nonsense," said George.

'George has always been a shade pig-headed. You can't drive him. I believe he had a secret idea that his wife worked the changes herself and that it was all some morbid hysterical plan of hers.

'Well, the fatal night came. Mrs Pritchard locked her door as usual. She was very calm—in almost an exalted state of mind. The nurse was worried by her state—wanted to give her a stimulant, an injection of strychnine, but Mrs Pritchard refused. In a way, I believe, she was enjoying herself. George said she was.'

'I think that's quite possible,' said Mrs Bantry. 'There must have been a strange sort of glamour about the whole thing.'

'There was no violent ringing of the bell the next morning. Mrs Pritchard usually woke about eight. When, at eight-thirty, there was no sign from her, nurse rapped loudly on the door. Getting no reply, she fetched George, and insisted on the door being broken open. They did so with the help of a chisel.

'One look at the still figure on the bed was enough for Nurse Copling. She sent George to telephone for the doctor, but it was too late. Mrs Pritchard, he said, must have been dead at least eight hours. Her smelling-salts lay by her hand on the bed, *and on the wall beside her one of the pinky-red geraniums was a bright deep blue.*'

'Horrible,' said Miss Helier with a shiver.

Sir Henry was frowning.

'No additional details?'

Colonel Bantry shook his head, but Mrs Bantry spoke quickly.

'The gas.'

'What about the gas?' asked Sir Henry.

'When the doctor arrived there was a slight smell of gas, and sure enough he found the gas ring in the fireplace very slightly turned on; but so little that it couldn't have mattered.'

'Did Mr Pritchard and the nurse not notice it when they first went in?'

'The nurse said she did notice a slight smell. George said he didn't notice gas, but something made him feel very queer and overcome; but he put it down to shock—and probably it was. At any rate there was no question of gas poisoning. The smell was scarcely noticeable.'

'And that's the end of the story?'

'No, it isn't. One way and another, there was a lot of talk. The servants, you see, had overheard things—had heard, for instance, Mrs Pritchard telling her husband that he hated her and would jeer if she were dying. And also more recent remarks. She had said one day, apropos of his refusing to leave the house: "Very well, when I am dead, I hope everyone will realize that you have killed me." And, as ill luck would have it, he had been mixing some weed killer for the garden paths the day before. One of the younger servants had seen him and had afterwards seen him taking up a glass of hot milk to his wife.

'The talk spread and grew. The doctor had given a certificate—I don't know exactly in what terms—shock, syncope, heart failure, probably some medical term meaning nothing much. However the poor lady had not been a month in her grave before an exhumation order was applied for and granted.'

'And the result of the autopsy was nil, I remember,' said Sir Henry gravely. 'A case, for once, of smoke without fire.'

'The whole thing is really very curious,' said Mrs Bantry. 'That fortune-teller, for instance—Zarida. At the address where she was supposed to be, no one had ever heard of any such person!'

'She appeared once—out of the blue,' said her husband, 'and then utterly vanished. Out of the *blue*—that's rather good!'

'And what is more,' continued Mrs Bantry, 'little Nurse Carstairs, who was supposed to have recommended her, had never even heard of her.'

They looked at each other.

'It's a mysterious story,' said Dr Lloyd. 'One can make guesses; but to guess—'

He shook his head.

'Has Mr Pritchard married Miss Instow?' asked Miss Marple in her gentle voice.

'Now why do you ask that?' inquired Sir Henry.

Miss Marple opened her gentle blue eyes.

'It seems to me so important,' she said. 'Have they married?'

Colonel Bantry shook his head.

'We—well, we expected something of the kind—but it's eighteen months now. I don't believe they even see much of each other.'

'That is important,' said Miss Marple. 'Very important.'

'Then you think the same as I do,' said Mrs Bantry. 'You think—'

'Now Dolly,' said her husband. 'It's unjustifiable—what you're going to say. You can't go about accusing people without a shadow of proof.'

'Don't be so—so manly, Arthur. Men are always afraid to say *anything*. Anyway, this is all between ourselves. It's just a wild fantastic idea of mine that possibly—only *possibly*—Jean Instow disguised herself as a fortune-teller. Mind you, she may have done it for a joke. I don't for a minute think that she meant any harm; but if she did do it, and if Mrs Pritchard was foolish enough to die of fright—well, that's what Miss Marple meant, wasn't it?'

'No, dear, not quite,' said Miss Marple. 'You see, if I were going to kill anyone—which, of course, I wouldn't dream of doing for a minute, because it would be very wicked, and besides I don't like killing—not even wasps, though I know it has to be, and I'm sure the gardener does it as humanely as possible. Let me see, what was I saying?'

'If you wished to kill anyone,' prompted Sir Henry.

'Oh yes. Well, if I did, I shouldn't be at all satisfied to trust to *fright*. I know one reads of people dying of it, but it seems a very uncertain sort of thing, and the most nervous people are far more brave than one really thinks they are. I should like something definite and certain, and make a thoroughly good plan about it.'

'Miss Marple,' said Sir Henry, 'you frighten me. I hope you will never wish to remove me. Your plans would be too good.'

Miss Marple looked at him reproachfully.

'I thought I had made it clear that I would never contemplate such wickedness,' she said. 'No, I was trying to put myself in the place of—er—a certain person.'

'Do you mean George Pritchard?' asked Colonel Bantry. 'I'll never believe it of George—though, mind you, even the nurse believes it. I went and saw her about a month afterwards, at the time of the exhumation. She didn't know how it was done—in fact, she wouldn't say anything at all—but it was clear enough that she believed George to be in some way responsible for his wife's death. She was convinced of it.'

'Well,' said Dr Lloyd, 'perhaps she wasn't so far wrong. And mind you, a nurse often *knows*. She can't say—she's got no proof—but she *knows*.'

Sir Henry leant forward.

'Come now, Miss Marple,' he said persuasively. 'You're lost in a daydream. Won't you tell us all about it?'

Miss Marple started and turned pink.

'I beg your pardon,' she said. 'I was just thinking about our District Nurse. A most difficult problem.'

'More difficult than the problem of the blue geranium?'

'It really depends on the primroses,' said Miss Marple. 'I mean, Mrs Bantry said they were yellow and pink. If it was a pink primrose that turned blue, of course, that fits in perfectly. But if it happened to be a yellow one—'

'It was a pink one,' said Mrs Bantry.

She stared. They all stared at Miss Marple.

'Then that seems to settle it,' said Miss Marple. She shook her head regretfully. 'And the wasp season and everything. And of course the gas.'

'It reminds you, I suppose, of countless village tragedies?' said Sir Henry.

'Not tragedies,' said Miss Marple. 'And certainly nothing criminal. But it does remind me a little of the trouble we are having with the District Nurse. After all, nurses are human beings, and what with having to be so correct in their behaviour and wearing those uncomfortable collars and being so thrown with the family—well, can you wonder that things sometimes happen?'

A glimmer of light broke upon Sir Henry.

'You mean Nurse Carstairs?'

'Oh no. Not Nurse Carstairs. Nurse *Copling*. You see, she had been there before, and very much thrown with Mr Pritchard, who you say is an attractive man. I daresay she thought, poor thing—well, we needn't go into that. I don't suppose she knew about Miss Instow, and of course afterwards, when she found out, it turned her against him and she tried to do all the harm she could. Of course the letter really gave her away, didn't it?'

'What letter?'

'Well, she wrote to the fortune-teller at Mrs Pritchard's request, and the fortune-teller came, apparently in answer to the letter. But later it was discovered that there never had been such a person at that address. So that shows that Nurse Copling was in it. She only pretended to write—so what could be more likely than that *she* was the fortune-teller herself?'

'I never saw the point about the letter,' said Sir Henry. 'That's a most important point, of course.'

'Rather a bold step to take,' said Miss Marple, 'because Mrs Pritchard might have recognized her in spite of the disguise—though of course if she had, the nurse could have pretended it was a joke.'

'What did you mean,' said Sir Henry, 'when you said that if you were a certain person you would not have trusted to fright?'

'One couldn't be *sure* that way,' said Miss Marple. 'No, I think that the warnings and the blue flowers were, if I may use a military term,' she laughed self-consciously—'just *camouflage.*'

'And the real thing?'

'I know,' said Miss Marple apologetically, 'that I've got wasps on the brain. Poor things, destroyed in their thousands—and usually on such a beautiful summer's day. But I remember thinking, when I saw the gardener shaking up the cyanide of potassium in a bottle with water, how like smelling-salts it looked. And if it were put in a smelling-salt bottle and substituted for the real one—well, the poor lady was in the habit of using her smelling-salts. Indeed you said they were found by her hand. Then, of course, while Mr Pritchard went to telephone to the doctor, the nurse would change it for the real bottle, and she'd just turn on the gas a little bit to mask any smell of almonds and in case anyone felt queer, and I always have heard that cyanide leaves no trace if you wait long enough. But, of course, I may be wrong, and it may have been something entirely different in the bottle; but that doesn't really matter, does it?'

Miss Marple paused, a little out of breath.

Jane Helier leant forward and said, 'But the blue geranium, and the other flowers?'

'Nurses always have litmus paper, don't they?' said Miss

Marple, 'for—well, for testing. Not a very pleasant subject. We won't dwell on it. I have done a little nursing myself.' She grew delicately pink. 'Blue turns red with acids, and red turns blue with alkalis. So easy to paste some red litmus over a red flower—near the bed, of course. And then, when the poor lady used her smelling-salts, the strong ammonia fumes would turn it blue. Really most ingenious. Of course, the geranium wasn't blue when they first broke into the room—nobody noticed it till afterwards. When nurse changed the bottles, she held the Sal Ammoniac against the wallpaper for a minute, I expect.'

'You might have been there, Miss Marple,' said Sir Henry.

'What worries me,' said Miss Marple, 'is poor Mr Pritchard and that nice girl, Miss Instow. Probably both suspecting each other and keeping apart—and life so very short.'

She shook her head.

'You needn't worry,' said Sir Henry. 'As a matter of fact I have something up my sleeve. A nurse has been arrested on a charge of murdering an elderly patient who had left her a legacy. It was done with cyanide of potassium substituted for smelling-salts. Nurse Copling trying the same trick again. Miss Instow and Mr Pritchard need have no doubts as to the truth.'

'Now isn't that nice?' cried Miss Marple. 'I don't mean about the new murder, of course. That's very sad, and shows how much wickedness there is in the world, and that if once you give way—which reminds me I *must* finish my little conversation with Dr Lloyd about the village nurse.'

THE STOLEN RUBENS

BY JACQUES FUTRELLE

Matthew Kale made fifty million dollars out of axle grease, after which he began to patronize the high arts. It was simple enough: he had the money, and Europe had the old masters. His method of buying was simplicity itself. There were five thousand square yards, more or less, in the huge gallery of his marble mansion which were to be covered, so he bought five thousand yards, more or less, of art. Some of it was good, some of it fair, and much of it bad. The chief picture in the collection was a Rubens, which he had picked up in Rome for fifty thousand dollars.

Soon after acquiring his collection, Kale decided to make certain alterations in the vast room where the pictures hung. They were all taken down and stored in the ballroom, equally vast, with their faces toward the wall. Meanwhile Kale and his family took refuge in a near-by hotel.

It was at this hotel that Kale met Jules de Lesseps. De Lesseps was distinctly the sort of Frenchman whose conversation resembles calisthenics. He was nervous, quick, and agile, and he told Kale in confidence that he was not only a painter himself, but a connoisseur in the high arts. Pompous in the pride of possession, Kale went to a good deal of trouble to exhibit his private collection for de Lesseps' delectation. It happened in the ballroom, and the true artist's delight shone in the Frenchman's eyes as he handled the pieces which were good. Some of the others made him smile, but it was an inoffensive sort of smile.

With his own hands Kale lifted the precious Rubens and held it before the Frenchman's eyes. It was a "Madonna and Child," one of those wonderful creations which have endured through the years with all the sparkle and color beauty of their pristine days. Kale seemed disappointed because de Lesseps was not particularly enthusiastic about this picture.

"Why, it's a Rubens!" he exclaimed.

"Yes, I see," replied de Lesseps.

"It cost me fifty thousand dollars."

"It is perhaps worth more than that," and the Frenchman shrugged his shoulders as he turned away.

Kale looked at him in chagrin. Could it be that de Lesseps did not understand that it was a Rubens, and that Rubens was a painter? Or was it that he had failed to hear him say that it cost him fifty thousand dollars? Kale was accustomed to seeing people bob their heads and open their eyes when he said fifty thousand dollars; therefore, "Don't you like it?" he asked.

"Very much indeed," replied de Lesseps; "but I have seen it before. I saw it in Rome just a week or so before you purchased it."

They rummaged on through the pictures, and at last a Whistler was turned up for their inspection. It was one of the famous Thames series, a water color. De Lesseps' face radiated excitement, and several times he glanced from the water color to the Rubens as if mentally comparing the exquisitely penciled and colored newer work with the bold, masterly technic of the older painting.

Kale misunderstood his silence. "I don't think much of this one myself," he explained apologetically. "It's a Whistler, and all that, and it cost me five thousand dollars, and I sort of had to have it, but still it isn't just the kind of thing that I like. What do you think of it?"

"I think it is perfectly wonderful!" replied the Frenchman enthusiastically. "It is the essence, the superlative, of Whistler's work. I wonder if it would be possible," and he turned to face Kale, "for me to make a copy of that? I have some slight skill in painting myself, and dare say I could make a fairly creditable copy of it."

Kale was flattered. He was more and more impressed each moment with the picture. "Why certainly," he replied. "I will have it sent up to the hotel, and you can—"

"No, no, no!" interrupted de Lesseps quickly. "I wouldn't care to accept the responsibility of having the picture in my charge. There is always a danger of fire. But if you would give me permission to come here—this room is large and airy and light—and besides it is quiet—"

"Just as you like," said Kale magnanimously. "I merely thought the other way would be most convenient for you."

De Lesseps laid one hand on the millionaire's arm. "My dear friend," he said earnestly, "if these pictures were my pictures, I shouldn't try to accommodate anybody where they were concerned. I dare say the collection as it stands cost you—"

"Six hundred and eighty-seven thousand dollars," volunteered Kale proudly.

"And surely they must be well protected here in your house during your absence."

"There are about twenty servants in the house, while the workmen are making the alterations," said Kale, "and three of them don't do anything but watch this room. No one can go in or out except by the door we entered—the others are locked and barred—and then only with my permission, or a written order from me. No sir, nobody can get away with anything in this room."

"Excellent—excellent!" said de Lesseps admiringly. He smiled a little. "I am afraid I did not give you credit for being the far-sighted businessman that you are." He turned and glanced over the collection of pictures abstractedly. "A clever thief, though," he ventured, "might cut a valuable painting, for instance the Rubens, out of the frame, roll it up, conceal it under his coat, and escape."

Kale laughed and shook his head.

It was a couple of days later at the hotel that de Lesseps brought up the subject of copying the Whistler. He was profuse in his thanks when Kale volunteered to accompany him into the mansion and witness the preliminary stages of the work. They paused at the ballroom door.

"Jennings," said Kale to the liveried servant there, "this is

Mr. de Lesseps. He is to come and go as he likes. He is going to do some work in the ballroom here. See that he isn't disturbed."

De Lesseps noticed the Rubens leaning carelessly against some other pictures, with the holy face of the Madonna turned toward them. "Really, Mr. Kale," he protested, "that picture is too valuable to be left about like that. If you will let your servants bring me some canvas, I shall wrap it and place it up on this table off the floor. Suppose there were mice here!"

Kale thanked him. The necessary orders were given, and finally the picture was carefully wrapped and placed beyond harm's reach, whereupon de Lesseps adjusted himself, paper, easel, stool, and all, and began his work of copying. There Kale left him.

Three days later Kale found the artist still at his labor.

"I just dropped by," he explained, "to see how the work in the gallery was getting along. It will be finished in another week. I hope I am not disturbing you?"

"Not at all," said de Lesseps; "I have nearly finished. See how I am getting along?" He turned the easel toward Kale.

The millionaire gazed from that toward the original which stood on a chair nearby, and frank admiration for the artist's efforts was in his eyes. "Why, it's fine!" he exclaimed. "It's just as good as the other one, and I bet you don't want any five thousand dollars for it—eh?"

That was all that was said about it at the time. Kale wandered about the house for an hour or so, then dropped into the ballroom where de Lesseps was getting his paraphernalia together, and they walked back to the hotel. The artist carried under one arm his copy of the Whistler, loosely rolled up.

Another week passed, and the workmen who had been engaged in refinishing and decorating the gallery had gone. De Lesseps volunteered to assist in the work of rehanging the pictures, and Kale gladly turned the matter over to him. It was in the afternoon of the day this work began that de Lesseps, chatting pleasantly with Kale, ripped loose the canvas which enshrouded the precious Rubens. Then he paused with an exclamation of dismay. The picture was gone; the frame which had held it was empty. A thin strip of canvas around the inside edge showed that a sharp penknife had been used to cut out the painting.

All of these facts came to the attention of Professor Augustus S. F. X. Van Dusen—The Thinking Machine. This was a day or so after Kale had rushed into Detective Mallory's office at police headquarters with the statement that his Rubens had been stolen. He banged his fist down on the detective's desk, and roared at him.

"It cost me fifty thousand dollars! Why don't you do something? What are you sitting there staring at me for?"

"Don't excite yourself, Mr. Kale," the detective advised. "I will put my men at work right now to recover the—the— What is a Rubens, anyway?"

"It's a picture!" bellowed Kale. "A piece of canvas with some paint on it, and it cost me fifty thousand dollars— don't you forget that!"

So the police machinery was set in motion to recover the picture. And in time the matter fell under the watchful eye of Hutchinson Hatch, reporter. He learned the facts preceding the disappearance of the picture and then called on de Lesseps. He found the artist in a state of excitement bordering on hysteria; an intimation from the reporter of the object of his visit caused de Lesseps to burst into words.

"*Mon Dieu!* It is outrageous! What can I do? I was the only one in the room for several days. I was the one who took such pains to protect the picture. And now it is gone! The loss is irreparable. What can I do?"

Hatch didn't have any very definite ideas as to just what he could do, so he let him go on. "As I understand it, Mr. de Lesseps," he interrupted at last, "no one else was in the room, except you and Mr. Kale, all the time you were there?"

"No one else."

"And I think Mr. Kale said that you were making a copy of some famous water color; weren't you?"

"Yes, a Thames scene by Whistler," was the reply. "That is it, hanging over the fireplace."

Hatch glanced at the picture admiringly. It was an exquisite copy, and showed the deft touch of a man who was himself an artist of great ability.

De Lesseps read the admiration in his face. "It is not bad," he said modestly. "I studied with Carolus Duran."

With all else that was known, and this little additional information, which seemed of no particular value to the reporter, the entire matter was laid before The Thinking

Machine. That distinguished man listened from beginning to end without comment.

"Who had access to that room?" he asked finally.

"That is what the police are working on now," said Hutchinson Hatch. "There are a couple of dozen servants in the house, and I suppose, in spite of Kale's rigid orders, there was a certain laxity in their enforcement."

"Of course that makes it more difficult," said The Thinking Machine in the perpetually irritated voice which was so characteristic a part of himself. "Perhaps it would be best for us to go to Mr. Kale's home and personally investigate."

Kale received them with the reserve which rich men usually show in the presence of representatives of the press. He stared frankly and somewhat curiously at the diminutive figure of the scientist, who explained the object of their visit.

"I guess you fellows can't do anything with this," the millionaire assured them. "I've got some regular detectives on it."

"Is Mr. Mallory here now?" asked The Thinking Machine curtly.

"Yes, he is upstairs in the servants' quarters."

"May we see the room from which the picture was taken?" inquired the scientist, with a suave intonation which Hatch knew well.

Kale granted the permission with a wave of the hand, and ushered them into the ballroom, where the pictures had been stored. From the center of this room The Thinking Machine surveyed it all. The windows were high. Half a dozen doors leading out into the hallways, the conservatory, quiet nooks of the mansion offered innumerable possibilities of access. After this one long comprehensive squint, The Thinking Machine went over and picked up the frame from which the Rubens had been cut. For a long time he examined it. Kale's impatience was evident. Finally the scientist turned to him.

"How well do you know M. de Lesseps?"

"I've known him for only a month or so. Why?"

"Did he bring you letters of introduction, or did you meet him merely casually?"

Kale regarded him with displeasure. "My own personal affairs have nothing whatever to do with this matter! Mr. De Lesseps is a gentleman of integrity, and certainly he is the last whom I would suspect of any connection with the disappearance of the picture."

"That is usually the case," remarked The Thinking Machine tartly. He turned to Hatch. "Just how good a copy was that he made of the Whistler picture?"

"I have never seen the original," Hatch replied; "but the workmanship was superb. Perhaps Mr. Kale wouldn't object to us seeing—"

"Oh, of course not," said Kale resignedly. "Come in; it's in the gallery."

Hatch submitted the picture to a careful scrutiny. "I should say the copy is well-nigh perfect," was his verdict.

"Of course, in its absence, I can't say exactly; but it is certainly a superb work."

The curtains of a wide door almost in front of them were thrown aside suddenly, and Detective Mallory entered. He carried something in his hand, but at sight of them concealed it behind him. Unrepressed triumph was in his face.

"Ah, professor, we meet often; don't we?" he said.

"This reporter here and his friend seem to be trying to drag de Lesseps into this affair somehow," Kale complained to the detective. "I don't want anything like that to happen. He is liable to go out and print anything. They always do."

The Thinking Machine glared at him unwaveringly for an instant, then extended his hand towards Mallory. "Where did you find it?" he asked.

"Sorry to disappoint you, professor," said the detective sarcastically, "but this is the time when you were a little too late," and he produced the object which he held behind him. "Here is your picture, Mr. Kale."

Kale gasped in relief and astonishment, and held up the canvas with both hands to examine it. "Fine!" he told the detective. "I'll see that you don't lose anything by this. Why, that thing cost me fifty thousand dollars!"

The Thinking Machine leaned forward to squint at the upper right-hand corner of the canvas. "Where did you find it?" he asked again.

"Rolled up tight, and concealed in the bottom of a trunk in the room of one of the servants," explained Mallory. "The servant's name is Jennings. He is now under arrest."

"Jennings!" exclaimed Kale. "Why, he has been with me for years."

"Did he confess?" asked the scientist imperturbably.

"Of course not," said Mallory. "He says some of the other servants must have hidden it there."

The Thinking Machine nodded at Hatch. "I think perhaps that is all," he remarked. "I congratulate you, Mr. Mallory, upon bringing the matter to such a quick and satisfactory conclusion."

Ten minutes later they left the house and took a taxi for the scientist's home. Hatch was a little chagrined at the unexpected termination of the affair.

"Mallory does show an occasional gleam of human intelligence, doesn't he?"

"Not that I ever noticed," remarked The Thinking Machine crustily.

"But he found the picture," Hatch insisted.

"Of course he found it. It was put there for him to find."

"Put there for him to find!" repeated the reporter. "Didn't Jennings steal it?"

"If he did, he's a fool."

"Well, if he didn't steal it, who put it there?"

"De Lesseps."

"De Lesseps!" echoed Hatch. "Why the deuce did he steal a fifty thousand dollar picture and put it in a servant's trunk to be found?"

The Thinking Machine twisted around in his seat and squinted at him coldly for a moment. "At times, Mr. Hatch,

I am absolutely amazed at your stupidity. I can understand it in a man like Mallory, but I have always given you credit for being an astute, quick-witted man."

Hatch smiled at the reproach. It was not the first time he had heard it. But nothing bearing on the problem in hand was said until they reached The Thinking Machine's house.

"The only real question in my mind, Mr. Hatch," said the scientist then, "is whether or not I should take the trouble to restore Mr. Kale's picture at all. He is perfectly satisfied, and will probably never know the difference. So—"

Suddenly Hatch saw something. "Great Scott!" he exclaimed. "Do you mean that the picture Mallory found was—"

"A copy of the original," snapped the scientist. "Personally I know nothing whatever about art; therefore, I could not say from observation that it is a copy, but I know it from the logic of the thing. When the original was cut from the frame, the knife swerved a little at the upper right-hand corner. The canvas remaining in the frame told me that. The picture that Mr. Mallory found did not correspond in this detail with the canvas in the frame. The conclusion is obvious."

"And de Lesseps has the original?"

"De Lesseps has the original. How did he get it? In any one of a dozen ways. He might have rolled it up and stuck it under his coat. He might have had a confederate. But I don't think that any ordinary method of theft would have appealed to him. I am giving him credit for being clever, as I must when we review the whole case.

"For instance, he asked for permission to copy the Whistler, which you saw was the same size as the Rubens. It was granted. He copied it practically under guard, always with the chance that Mr. Kale himself would drop in. It took him three days to copy it, so he says. He was alone in the room all that time. He knew that Mr. Kale had not the faintest idea of art. Taking advantage of that, what would have been simpler than to have copied the Rubens in oil? He could have removed it from the frame immediately after he canvased it over, and kept it in a position near him where it could be quickly concealed if he was interrupted. Remember, the picture is worth fifty thousand dollars; therefore, was worth the trouble.

"De Lesseps is an artist—we know that—and dealing with a man who knew nothing whatever of art, he had no fears. We may suppose his idea all along was to use the copy of the Rubens as a sort of decoy after he got away with the original. You saw that Mallory didn't know the difference, and it was safe for him to suppose that Mr. Kale wouldn't. His only danger until he could get away gracefully was of some critic or connoisseur, perhaps, seeing the copy. His boldness we see readily in the fact that he permitted himself to discover the theft; that he discovered it after he had vol-unteered to assist Mr. Kale in the general work of rehanging the pictures in the gallery. Just how he put the picture in Jennings' trunk I don't happen to know. We can imagine many ways." He lay back in his chair for a minute without speaking, eyes steadily turned upward, fingers placed precisely tip to tip.

"But how did he take the picture from the Kale home?" asked Hatch.

"He took it with him probably under his arm the day he left the house with Mr. Kale," was the astonishing reply.

Hatch was staring at him in amazement. After a moment the scientist rose and passed into the adjoining room, and the telephone bell there jingled. When he joined Hatch again he picked up his hat and they went out together.

De Lesseps was in when their cards were sent up, and received them. They conversed about the case generally for ten minutes, while the scientist's eyes were turned inquiringly here and there about the room. At last there came a knock on the door.

"It is Detective Mallory, Mr. Hatch," remarked The Thinking Machine. "Open the door for him."

De Lesseps seemed startled for just one instant, then quickly recovered. Mallory's eyes were full of questions when he entered.

"I should like, Mr. Mallory," began The Thinking Machine quietly, "to call your attention to this copy of Mr. Kale's picture by Whistler—over the mantel here. Isn't it excellent? You have seen the original?"

Mallory grunted. De Lesseps' face, instead of expressing appreciation of the compliment, blanched, and his hands closed tightly. Again he recovered himself and smiled.

"The beauty of this picture lies not only in its faithfulness to the original," the scientist went on, "but also in the fact that it was painted under extraordinary circumstances. For instance, I don't know if you know, Mr. Mallory, that it is possible so to combine glue and putty and a few other commonplace things into a paste which will effectually blot out an oil painting, and offer at the same time an excellent surface for water color work!"

There was a moment's pause, during which the three men stared at him silently—with conflicting emotions.

"This water color—this copy of Whistler," continued the scientist evenly—"is painted on such a paste as I have described. That paste in turn covers the original Rubens picture. It can be removed with water without damage to the picture, which is in oil, so that instead of a copy of the Whistler painting, we have an original by Rubens, worth fifty thousand dollars. That is true; isn't it, M. de Lesseps?"

There was no reply to the question—none was needed.

It was an hour later, after de Lesseps was safely in his cell, that Hatch called up The Thinking Machine and asked one question.

"How did you know that the water color was painted over the Rubens?"

"Because it was the only absolutely safe way in which the Rubens could be hopelessly lost to those who were looking for it, and at the same time perfectly preserved," was the answer. "I told you de Lesseps was a clever man, and a little logic did the rest. Two and two always make four, Mr. Hatch, not sometimes, but all the time."

ASK ME ANOTHER

BY FRANK GRUBER

Oliver Quade was reading the morning paper, his bare feet on the bed and his chair tilted back against the radiator. Charlie Boston was on the bed, wrapped to his chin in a blanket and reading a copy of *Exciting Confessions*.

It was just a usual, peaceful, after-breakfast interlude in the lives of Oliver Quade, the Human Encyclopedia, and Charlie Boston, his friend and assistant.

And then Life intruded itself upon the bit of Utopia. Life in the form of the manager of the Eagle Hotel. He beat a tattoo upon the thin panels of the door. Quade put down his newspaper and sighed.

"Charles, will you please open the door and let in the wolf?"

Charlie Boston unrolled himself from the blanket. He scowled at Quade. "You think it's the manager about the room rent?"

"Of course, it is. Let him in before he breaks down the door."

It was the manager. In his right fist he held a ruled form on which were scrawled some unpleasant figures. "About your rent, Mr. Quade," he said severely. "We must have the money today."

Quade looked at the manager of the Eagle Hotel, a

puzzled expression on his face. "Rent? Money?"

"Of course," snapped the manager. "This is the third time this week I've asked for it."

A light came into Quade's eyes. He made a quick movement and his feet and the front legs of the chair hit the carpeted floor simultaneously.

"Charles!" he roared in a voice that shook the room and caused the hotel manager to cringe. "Did you forget to get that money from the bank and pay this little bill?"

Charlie Boston took up Quade's cue.

"Gosh, I'm awful sorry. On my way to the bank yesterday afternoon I ran into our old friend John Belmont of New York and he dragged me into the Palmer House Bar for a cocktail. By the time I could tear myself away, the bank was closed."

Quade raised his hands and let them fall hopelessly. "You see, Mr. Creighton, I just can't trust him to do anything. Now I've got to go out into the cold this morning and get it myself."

The hotel manager's eyes glinted. "Listen, you've stalled—" he began, but Quade suddenly stabbed out a hand toward him. "That reminds me, Mr. Creighton, I've a couple of complaints to make. We're not getting enough heat here and last night the damfool next door kept us awake half the night with his radio. I want you to see that he keeps quiet tonight. And do something about the heat. I can't stand drafty, cold rooms."

The manager let out a weary sigh. "All right, I'll look after it. But about that rent—"

"Yes, of course," cut in Quade, "and your maid left only two towels this morning. Please see that a couple more are sent up. Immediately!"

The manager closed the door behind him with a bang. Oliver Quade chuckled and lifted his newspaper again. But Charlie Boston wouldn't let him read.

"You got away with it, Ollie," he said, "but it's the last time. I know it. I'll bet we get locked out before tonight." He shook his head sadly. "You, Oliver Quade, with the greatest brain in captivity, are you going to walk the streets tonight in ten below zero weather?"

"Of course not, Charles," sighed Quade. "I was just about to tell you that we're going out to make some money today. Look, it's here in this paper. The Great Chicago Auditorium Poultry Show."

Boston's eyes lit up for a moment, but then dimmed again. "Can we raise three weeks' rent at a poultry show?"

Quade slipped his feet into his socks and shoes. "That remains to be seen. This paper mentions twenty thousand paid admissions. Among that many people there ought to be a few who are interested in higher learning. Well, are you ready?"

Boston went to the clothes closet and brought out their overcoats and a heavy suitcase. Boston was of middle height and burly. He could bend iron bars with his muscular hands. Quade was taller and leaner. His face was hawk-like, his nose a little too pointed and lengthy, but few ever noticed that. They saw only his piercing, sparkling eyes and felt his dominant personality.

The auditorium was almost two miles from their hotel, but lacking carfare, Quade and Boston walked. When they reached their destination, Quade cautioned Boston:

"Be sharp now, Charlie. Act like we belonged."

Quade opened the outer door and walked blithely past the ticket windows to the door leading into the auditorium proper. A uniformed man at the door held out his hand for the tickets.

"Hello," Quade said, heartily. "How're you today?"

"Uh, all right, I guess," replied the ticket-taker. "You boys got passes?"

"Oh, sure. We're just taking in some supplies for the breeders. Brrr! It's cold today. Well, be seeing you." And with that he breezed past the ticket-taker.

"H'are ya, pal," Boston said, treading on Quade's heels.

The auditorium was a huge place but even so, it was almost completely filled with row upon row of wire exhibition coops, each coop containing a feathered fowl of some sort.

"What a lot of gumps!" Boston observed.

"Don't use that word around here," Quade cautioned. "These poultry folks take their chickens seriously. Refer to the chickens as 'fine birds' or 'elegant fowls' or something like that...Damn these publicity men!"

"Huh?"

Quade waved a hand about the auditorium. "The paper said twenty thousand paid admissions. How many people do you see in here?"

Boston craned his neck around. "If there's fifty I'm

countin' some of 'em twice. How the hell can they pay the nut with such a small attendance?"

"The entry fees. There must be around two thousand chickens in here and the entry fee for each chicken is at least a dollar and a half. The prize money doesn't amount to much and I guess the paid admissions are velvet—if they get any, which I doubt."

"Twenty thousand, bah!" snorted Boston. "Well, do we go back?"

"Where? Our only chance was to stay in our room. I'll bet the manager changed the lock the minute we left it."

"So what?"

"So I get to work. For the dear old Eagle Hotel."

Quade ploughed through an aisle to the far end of the auditorium. Commercial exhibits were contained in booths all around the four sides of the huge room, but Quade found a small spot that had been overlooked and pushed a couple of chicken coops into the space.

Then he climbed up on the coops and began talking.

The Human Encyclopedia's voice was an amazing one. People who heard it always marveled that such a tremendous voice could come from so lean a man. Speaking without noticeable effort, his voice rolled out across the chicken coops.

"I'm Oliver Quade, the Human Encyclopedia," he boomed. "I have the greatest brain in the entire country. I know the answers to all questions, what came first, the chicken or the egg, every historical date since the beginning of time, the population of every city in the country, how to eradicate mice in your poultry yards, how to mix feeds to make your chickens lay more eggs. Everything. Everything under the sun. On any subject; history, science, agriculture and mathematics."

The scattered persons in the auditorium began to converge upon Quade's stand. Inside of two minutes three-fourths of the people in the building were gathered before Quade and the rest were on their way. He continued his preliminary build-up in his rich, powerful voice.

"Ask me a question, someone. Let me prove that I'm the Human Encyclopedia, the man who knows the answers to all questions. Try me out, someone, on any subject; history, science, mathematics, agriculture—anything at all!"

Quade stabbed out his lean forefinger at a middle-aged, sawed-off man wearing a tan smock. "You, sir, ask me a question?"

The man flushed at being singled out of the crowd. "Why, uh, I don't know of any…Yes, I do. What's the highest official egg record ever made by a hen?"

"That's the stuff," smiled Quade. He held out his hand dramatically. "That's a good question, but an easy one to answer. The highest record ever made by a hen in an American official egg-laying contest is three hundred and forty-two eggs. It was made in 1930 at the Athens, Georgia, Egg-Laying Contest, by a Single-Comb White Leghorn. Am I right, Mister?"

The sawed-off man nodded grudgingly. "Yeah, but I don't see how you knew it. Most poultry folks don't even remember it."

"Oh, but you forget I told you I had the greatest brain in the country. I know the answers to all questions on any subject. Don't bother to ask me simple poultry questions. Try me on something hard. You—" he picked out a lean, dour looking man. "Ask me something hard."

The man bit his lip a moment, then said:

"All right, what State has the longest coast line?"

Quade grinned. "Ah, you're trying the tricky stuff. But you can't fool me. Most folks would say California or Florida. But the correct answer is Michigan. And to head off the rest of you on the trick geography questions let me say right away that Kentucky has the largest number of other States touching it and Minnesota has the farthest northern point of any State. Next question!"

A young fellow wearing pince-nez put his tongue into his cheek and asked,

"Why and how does a cat purr?"

"Oh-oh!" Quade craned his neck to stare at the young fellow. "I see we have a student with us. Well, young man, you've asked a question so difficult that practically every university professor in this country would be stumped on it. But I'm not. It so happens that I read a recent paper by Professor E. L. Gibbs of the Harvard Medical School in which he gave the results of his experiments on four hundred cats to learn the answer to that very same question. The first part of the question is simple enough—the cat purrs when it is contented, but to explain the actual act of purring is a little more difficult. Contentment in a cat relaxes the infundicular nerve in the brain, which reacts upon the pituitary and bronchial organs and makes the purring sound issue from the cat's throat…Try that one on your friends, sometime. Someone else try me on a question."

"I'd like to ask one," said a clear, feminine voice. Quade's eyes lit up. He had already noticed the girl, the only female in his audience. She was amazingly pretty, the type of girl he would scarcely have expected to find at a poultry show. She was young, not more than twenty-one, and she had the finest chiseled features Quade had ever seen. She was a blonde and the rakish green hat and green coat she wore, although inexpensive, looked exceedingly well on her.

"Yes, what is the question?" he asked, leaning forward a bit.

The girl's chin came up defiantly. "I just want to know why certain poultry judges allow dyed birds to be judged for prizes!"

A sudden rumble went up in the crowd and Quade saw the sawed-off man in the tan smock whirl and glare angrily at the girl.

"Oh-oh," Quade said. "You seem to have asked a delicate question. Well, I'll answer it just the same. Any judge who allows a dyed Rhode Island Red to stay in the class is either an ignorant fool—or a crook!"

"Damn you!" roared the little man, turning back to Quade. "You can't say that to me. I'll—I'll have you thrown out of here." He started pushing his way through the crowd, heading in the direction of the front office.

"If the shoe fits, put it on," Quade called after him. Then to the girl: "Who's he?"

"A judge here. Stone's his name."

"Well, let's go on with the show," Quade said to the crowd. "Next question?"

Quade had lost nothing by his bold answer to the girl's question. The audience warmed to him and the questions came fast and furious.

"Who was the eleventh president of the United States?"

"What is the Magna Charta?"

"Who was the 1896 Olympic 220-meter champion?"

"How do you cure scaly legs in chickens?"

"How far is Saturn from the earth?"

Quade answered all questions put to him, with lightning rapidity. But suddenly he called a dramatic halt. "That's all the questions, folks. Now let me show you how you can learn all the answers yourselves to every question that has just been asked—and ten thousand more."

He held out his hands and Charlie Boston tossed a thick book into them which he had taken from the suitcase they had brought with them. Quade began ruffling the pages.

"They're all in here. This, my friends, is the 'Compendium of Human Knowledge,' the greatest book of its kind ever published. Twelve hundred pages, crammed with facts, information every one of you should know. The knowledge of the ages, condensed, classified, abbreviated. A complete high-school education in one volume. Ten minutes a day and this book will make you the most learned person in your community."

Quade lowered his voice to a confidential pitch. "Friends, I'm going to astonish you by telling you the most ridiculous thing you've ever heard: The price of this book. What do you think I'm asking for it? Twenty-five dollars? No, not even twenty…or fifteen. In fact, not even ten or five dollars. Just a mere, paltry, insignificant two dollars and ninety-five cents. But I'm only going to offer these books once at that price. Two-ninety-five, and here I come!"

Quade leaped down from his platform to attack his audience, supposedly built up to the buying pitch. But he was destined not to sell any books just then. Charlie Boston tugged at his coat sleeve.

"Look, Ollie!" he whispered hoarsely. "He got the cops!"

Quade raised himself to his toes to look over the chicken coops. He groaned. For the short man in the tan smock was coming up the center aisle leading a small procession of policemen.

Quade sighed. "Put the books back into the suitcase, Charlie." He leaned against a poultry coop and waited to submit quietly to the arrest.

But the policemen did not come toward him. Reaching the center aisle the man in the tan smock wheeled to the left, away from Quade, and the police followed him.

Quade's audience saw the police. Two or three persons broke away and started toward the other side of the building. The movement started a stampede and in a moment Charlie Boston and Quade were left alone.

"Something seems to have happened over there," Quade observed. "Wonder what?"

"From the mob of cops I'd say a murder," Boston replied dryly.

The word "murder" was scarcely out of Boston's mouth than it was hurled back at them from across the auditorium.

"It *is* a murder!" Quade gasped.

"This is no place for us, then," cried Boston. "Let's scram!"

He caught up the suitcase containing the books and started off. But Quade called him back. "That's no good. There's a cop at the door. We'll have to stick."

"Chickens!" howled Boston. "The minute you mentioned them at the hotel I had a hunch that something was going to happen. And I'll bet a plugged dime, which I haven't got, that we get mixed up in it."

"Maybe so, Charlie. But if I know cops there's going to be a lot of questioning and my hunch is that we'll be better off if we're not too upstage. Let's go over and find out what's what."

He started toward the other side of the auditorium. Boston followed, lugging the suitcase and grumbling.

All of the crowd had gathered in front of a huge, mahogany cabinet—a mammoth incubator. The door of the machine was standing open and two or three men were moving around inside.

Quade drew in his breath sharply when he saw the huddled body lying on the floor just inside the door of the incubator. Gently he began working his way through the crowd until he stood in front of the open incubator door.

The small group came out of the incubator and a beetle-browed man in a camel's hair overcoat and Homburg hat squared himself off before the girl in the green hat and coat. The man in the tan smock, his head coming scarcely up to the armpits of the big man, hopped around like a bantam rooster.

"I understand you had a quarrel with him yesterday," the big man said to the girl. "What about?"

The girl drew herself up to her full height. "Because his birds were dyed and the judge—the man behind you— refused to throw them out. That's why!"

The bantam spluttered. "She—why, that's a damn lie!"

The big detective turned abruptly, put a ham-like hand against the chest of the runt and shoved him back against the incubator with so much force that the little man gasped in pain.

"Listen, squirt," the detective said. "Nothing's been proved against this girl and until it is, she's a lady. Up here we don't call ladies liars."

He turned back to the girl and said with gruff kindness, "Now, Miss, let's have the story."

"There's no story," declared the girl. "I did quarrel with him, just like I did with Judge Stone. But—but I haven't seen Mr. Tupper since yesterday evening. That's all I can tell you because it's all I know."

"Yesterday, huh." The detective looked around the circle. "Anybody see him here today?"

"Yes, of course," said a stocky man of about forty-five. "I was talking to him early this morning, before the place was opened to the public. There were a dozen or more of us around then."

"You're the boss of this shebang?"

"Not exactly. Our poultry association operates this show. I'm Leo Cassmer, the secretary, and I'm in charge of the exhibits, if that's what you mean."

"Yeah, that's what I mean," replied the detective. "You're the boss. You know these exhibitors then. All right, who were here early this morning when this Tupper fellow was around?"

Cassmer, the show secretary, rubbed his chin. "Why, there was myself, Judge Stone, Ralph Conway, the Wyandotte man, Judge Welheimer and several of the men who work around here."

"And Miss Martin—was she here?"

"She came in before the place was officially opened, but she wasn't around the last time I saw Tupper."

"Who're Welheimer and Conway?"

A tall, silver-haired man stepped out of the crowd. "Conway's my name."

"And the judge?" persisted the detective.

A long-nosed man with a protruding lower lip came grudgingly out of the crowd. "I'm Judge Welheimer."

"You a real judge or just a chicken judge?"

"Why, uh, just a poultry judge. Licensed by the National Poultry Association."

"And you don't hold any public office at all? You're not even a justice of the peace?"

The long-nosed chicken judge reddened. He shook his head.

The detective's eyes sparkled. "That's fine. All that talk

about judges had me worried for a bit. But listen, you chicken judges and the rest of you. I'm Sergeant Dickinson of the Homicide Squad of this town. There's been a murder committed here and I'm investigating it. Which means I'm boss around here. Get me?"

Quade couldn't quite restrain a snicker. The sergeant's sharp ears heard it and he singled out Quade.

"And who the hell are you?"

"Oliver Quade, the Human Encyclopedia," Quade replied glibly. "I know the answers to all questions—"

Sergeant Dickinson's face twisted. "Ribbing me, ha? Step up here where I can get a good look at you."

Quade remained where he was. "There's a dead man in there. I don't like to get too close to dead people."

The sergeant took a half step toward Quade, but then stopped himself. He tried to smooth out his face, but it was still dark with anger.

"I'll get around to you in a minute, fella." He turned belligerently to the show secretary. "You, who found the body?"

Cassmer pointed to a pasty-faced young fellow of about thirty. The man grinned sickly.

"Yeah, I got in kinda late and started straightening things around. Then I saw that someone had stuck in that long staple in the door latch. I didn't think much about it and opened the door and there—there he was lying on the floor. Deader'n a mackerel!"

"You work for this incubator company?" the sergeant asked.

The young fellow nodded. "I'm the regional sales manager. Charge of this exhibit. It's the finest incubator on the market. Used by the best breeders and hatcherymen—"

"Can the sales talk," growled the detective. "*I'm* not going to buy one. Let's go back on your story. What made you say this man was murdered?"

"What else could it be? He was dead and the door was locked on the outside."

"I know that. But couldn't he have died of heart failure? There's plenty of air in that thing and besides there's a ventilator hole open up there."

"He was murdered," said Quade.

Sergeant Dickinson whirled. "And how do *you* know?"

"By looking at the body. Anyone could tell it was murder."

"Oh yeah. Maybe you'll tell me *how* he was killed. There ain't a mark on his body."

"No marks of violence, because he wasn't killed that way. He was killed with a poison gas. Something containing cyanogen."

The sergeant clamped his jaws together. "Go on! Who killed him?"

Quade shook his head. "No, that's your job. I've given you enough to start with."

"You've been very helpful," said the sergeant. "So much so that I'm going to arrest you!"

Charlie Boston groaned into Quade's ears. "Won't you ever learn to keep your mouth shut?"

But Quade merely grinned insolently. "If you arrest me I'll sue you for false arrest."

"I'll take a chance on that," said the detective. "No one could know as much as you do and not have had something to do with the murder."

"You're being very stupid, Sergeant," Quade said. "These men told you they hadn't seen Tupper alive for several hours. He's been dead at least three. And I just came into this building fifteen minutes ago."

"He's right," declared Anne Martin. "I saw him come in. He and his friend. They went straight over to the other side of the building and started that sales talk."

"What sales talk?"

The little poultry judge hopped in again. "He's a damn pitchman. Pulls some phony question and answer stuff and insults people. Claims he's the smartest man in the world. Bah!"

"Bah to you," said Quade.

"Cut it," cried Sergeant Dickinson. "I want to get the straight of this. You," he turned to Cassmer. "Did he really come in fifteen minutes ago?"

Cassmer shrugged. "I never saw him until a few minutes ago. But there's the ticket-taker. He'd know."

The ticket-taker, whose post had been taken over by a policeman, frowned. "Yeah, he came in just a little while ago. I got plenty reason to remember. Him and his pal crashed the gate. On *me!* First time anyone crashed the gate on me in eight years. But he was damn slick. He—"

"Never mind the details," sighed Sergeant Dickinson. "I can imagine he was slick about it. Well, Mister, you didn't kill him. But tell me—how the hell do you know he was gassed with cy—cyanide?"

"Cyanogen. It's got prussic acid in it. All right, the body was found inside the incubator, the door locked on the outside. That means someone locked him inside the incubator. The person who killed him. Right so far?"

"I'm listening." There was a thoughtful look in the sergeant's eyes.

"There's broken glass inside the incubator. The killer heaved in a bottle containing the stuff and slammed the door shut and locked it. The man inside was killed inside of a minute."

"Wait a minute. The glass is there all right, but how d'you know it contained cyanogen? There's no smell in there."

"No, because the killer opened the ventilator hole and turned on the electric fans inside the incubator. All that can be done from the outside. The fans cleared out the fumes. Simple."

"Not so simple. You still haven't said how you know it was cyanogen."

"Because he's got all the symptoms. Look at the body— pupils dilated, eyes wide, froth on the mouth, face livid, body twisted and stiff. That means he had convulsions. Well, if those symptoms don't mean cyanogen, I don't know what it's all about."

"Mister," said the detective. "Who did you say you were?"

"Oliver Quade, the Human Encyclopedia. I know everything."

"You know, I'm beginning to believe you. Well then, who did the killing?"

"That's against the union rules. I told you how the man was killed. Finding who did it is your job."

"All right, but tell me one thing more. If this cyanogen has prussic acid in it, it's a deadly poison. Folks can't usually buy it."

"City folks, you mean. Cyanogen is the base for several insecticides. I don't think this was pure cyanogen. I'm inclined to believe it was a diluted form, probably a gas used to kill rats on poultry farms. Any poultry raiser could buy that."

"Here comes the coroner's man," announced Detective Dickinson. "Now, we'll get a check on you, Mr. Quade."

Dr. Bogle, the coroner's physician, made a rapid, but thorough examination of the body. His announcement coincided startlingly with Quade's diagnosis.

"Prussic acid or cyanide. He inhaled it. Died inside of five minutes. About three and a half hours ago."

Quade's face was twisted in a queer smile. He walked off from the group. Charlie Boston and Anne Martin, the girl, followed.

"Do you mind my saying that you just performed some remarkable work?" the girl said admiringly.

"No, I don't mind your saying so," Quade grinned. "I *was* rather colossal."

"He pulls those things out of a hat," groused Boston. "He's a very smart man. Only one thing he can't do."

"What's that?"

Boston started to reply, but Quade's fierce look silenced him. Quade coughed. "Well, look—a hot dog stand. Reminds me, it's about lunch time. Feel like a hot dog and orangeade, Anne?"

The girl smiled at his familiarity. "I don't mind. I'm rather hungry."

Boston sidled up to Quade. "Hey, you forgot!" he whispered. "You haven't got any money."

Quade said, "Three dogs and orangeades!"

A minute later they were munching hot dogs. Quade finished his orangeade and half-way through the sandwich suddenly snapped his fingers.

"That reminds me, I forgot something. Excuse me a moment..." He started off suddenly toward the group around the incubator, ignoring Charlie Boston's startled protest.

Boston suddenly had no appetite. He chewed the food in his mouth as long as he could. The girl finished her sandwich and smiled at him.

"That went pretty good. Guess I'll have another. How about you?"

Boston almost choked. "Uh, no, I ain't hungry."

The girl ordered another hot dog and orangeade and finished them while Boston still fooled with the tail end of his first sandwich.

The concessionaire mopped up the counter all around Boston and Anne Martin and finally said, "That's eighty cents, Mister!"

Boston put the last of the sandwich in his mouth and began going through his pockets. The girl watched him curiously. Boston went through his pockets a second time. "That's funny," he finally said. "I must have left my wallet at the hotel. Quade…"

"Let me pay for it," said the girl, snapping open her purse.

Boston's face was as red as a Harvard beet. Such things weren't embarrassing to Quade, but they were to Boston.

"There's Mr. Quade," said Anne Martin. "Shall we join him?"

Boston was glad to get away from the hot dog stand.

The investigation was still going on. Sergeant Dickinson was on his hands and knees inside the incubator. A policeman stood at the door of it and a couple more were going over the exterior.

Quade saluted them with a piece of wire. "They're looking for clues," he said.

The girl shivered. "I'd like it much better if they'd take away Exhibit A."

"Can't. Not until they take pictures. I hear the photographers and the fingerprint boys are coming down. It's not really necessary either. Because I know who the murderer is!"

The girl gasped: "Who?"

Quade did not reply. He looked at the piece of wire in his hands. It was evidently a spoke from a wire poultry coop, but it had been twisted into an elongated question mark. He tapped Dickinson's shoulder with the wire.

The sergeant looked up and scowled. "Huh?"

"Want this?" Quade asked.

"What the hell is it?"

"Just a piece of wire I picked up."

"What're you trying to do, rib me?"

Quade shrugged. "No, but I saw you on your hands and knees and thought you were looking for something. Thought this might be it."

Dickinson snorted. "What the hell, if you're not going to tell me who did the killing let me alone."

"O.K." Quade flipped the piece of wire over a row of chicken coops. "Come," he said to Boston and Anne Martin. "Let's go look at the turkeys at the other end of the building."

Boston shuffled up beside Quade as the three walked through an aisle. "Who did it, Ollie?"

"Can't tell now, because I couldn't prove it. In a little while, perhaps."

Boston let out his pent-up breath. "If you ain't the damnedest guy ever!"

Anne Martin said, "You mean you're not going to tell Sergeant Dickinson?"

"Oh yes, but I'm going to wait a while. Maybe he'll tumble himself and I'd hate to deprive him of that pleasure...What time is it?"

"I don't know," Boston said. "I lost my watch in Kansas City. You remember that, don't you, Ollie?"

Quade winced. Boston had "lost" his watch in Uncle Ben's Three Gold Ball Shop. Quade's had gone to Uncle Moe in St. Louis.

"It's twelve-thirty," the girl said, looking at her wrist watch.

Quade nodded. "That's fine. The early afternoon editions of the papers will have accounts of the murder and a lot of morbid folks will flock around here later on. That means I can put on a good pitch and sell some of my books."

"I wanted to ask you about that," said Anne Martin. "You answered some really remarkable questions this morning. I don't for the life of me see how you do it."

"Forsaking modesty for the moment, I do it because I really know all the answers."

"All?"

"Uh-huh. You see, I've read an entire encyclopedia from cover to cover four times."

Anne looked at him in astonishment. "An entire encyclopedia?"

"Twenty-four volumes…Well, let's go back now. Charlie, keep your eyes open."

"Ah!" Charlie Boston said.

Dr. Bogle's men were just taking away the body of the murdered man. Sergeant Dickinson, a disgusted look on his face, had rounded up his men and was on the verge of leaving.

"Not going, Captain Dickinson?" Quade asked.

"What good will it do me to hang around?" snorted the sergeant. "Everyone and his brother has some phony alibi."

"But your clues, man?"

"What clues?"

Quade shook his head in exasperation. "I told you how the murder was committed, didn't I?"

"Yeah, sure, the guy locked the bloke in the incubator and tossed in the bottle of poison gas, then opened the ventilator and turned on the fans. But there were more than a dozen guys around and almost any one of them could have done it, without any of the others even noticing what he was doing."

"'No, you're wrong. Only one person could have done it."

A hush suddenly fell upon the crowd. Charlie Boston, tensed and crouching, was breathing heavily. The police sergeant's face became bleak. Quade had demonstrated his remarkable deductive ability a while ago and Dickinson was willing to believe anything of him, now.

Quade stepped lazily to a poultry coop, took hold of a wire bar and with a sudden twist tore it off. Then he stepped to the side of the incubator.

"Look at this ventilator," he said. "Notice that I can reach it easily enough. So could you, Lieutenant. We're about the same height—five feet ten. But a man only five-two couldn't reach it even by standing on his toes. Do you follow me?"

"Go on," said Sergeant Dickinson.

Quade twisted the piece of wire into an elongated question mark. "To move a box or chair up here and climb up on it would be to attract attention," he went on, "so the killer used a piece of wire to open the ventilator. Like this!" Quade caught the hook in the ventilator and pulled it open easily.

"That's good enough for me!" said Sergeant Dickinson. "You practically forced that wire on me a while ago and I couldn't see it. Well—*Judge Stone, you're under arrest!*"

"He's a liar!" roared the bantam poultry judge. "He can't prove anything like that on me. He just tore that piece of wire from that coop!"

"That's right," said Quade. "You saw me pick up the original piece of wire and when I threw it away after trying to give it to the sergeant you got it and disposed of it."

"You didn't *see* me."

"No, I purposely walked away to give you a chance to get rid of the wire. But I laid a trap for you. While I had that wire I smeared some ink on it to prove you handled it. Look at your hands, Judge Stone!"

Judge Stone raised both palms upward. His right thumb and fingers were smeared with a black stain.

Sergeant Dickinson started toward the little poultry judge. But the bantam uttered a cry of fright and darted away.

"Ha!" cried Charlie Boston and lunged for him. He wrapped his thick arms around the little man and tried to hold on to him. But the judge was suddenly fighting for his life. He clawed at Boston's face and kicked his shins furiously. Boston howled and released his grip to defend himself with his fists.

The poultry judge promptly butted Boston in the stomach and darted under his flailing arms.

It was Anne Martin who stopped him. As the judge

scrambled around Boston she stepped forward and thrust out her right foot. The little man tripped over it and plunged headlong to the concrete floor of the auditorium. Before he could get up Charlie Boston was on him. Sergeant Dickinson swooped down, a Police Positive in one hand and a pair of handcuffs in the other. The killer was secured.

Stone quit then. "Yes, I killed him, the damned lousy blackmailer. For years I judged his chickens at the shows and always gave him the edge. Then he double-crossed me, got me fired."

"What job?" asked Dickinson.

"My job as district manager for the Sibley Feed Company," replied Stone.

"Why'd he have you fired?" asked Quade. "Because you were short-weighing him on his feed? Is that it?"

"I gave him prizes his lousy chickens should never have had," snapped the little killer. "What if I did short-weigh him twenty or thirty per cent? I more than made up for it."

"Twenty or thirty per cent," said Quade, "would amount to quite a bit of money in the course of a year. In his advertising in the poultry papers Tupper claimed he raised over eight thousand chickens a year."

"I don't need any more," said Sergeant Dickinson. "Well, Mr. Quade, you certainly delivered the goods."

"Not me, I only told you who the murderer was. If it hadn't been for Miss Martin, he'd have got away."

Quade turned away. "Anne," he said, "Charlie and I are

90

flat broke. But this afternoon a flock of rubbernecks are going to storm this place and I'm going to take quite a chunk of money from them. But in the meantime...That hot dog wasn't very filling and I wonder if you'd stake us to a lunch?"

Anne Martin's eyes twinkled. "Listen, Mr. Quade, if you asked me for every cent I've got I'd give it to you right away—because you'd get it from me anyway, if you really wanted it. You're the world's greatest salesman. You even sold Judge Stone into confessing."

Quade grinned. "Yes? How?"

She pointed at Quade's hands. "You handled that first wire hook with your bare hands. How come *your* hands didn't get black?"

Quade chuckled. "Smart girl. Even the sergeant didn't notice that. Well, I'll confess. I saw the smudge on Judge Stone's hands away back when I was putting on my pitch. He must have used a leaky fountain pen or something."

"Then you didn't put anything on it?"

"No. But *I* knew he was the murderer and *he* knew it... only he didn't know his hands were dirty. So..."

The girl drew a deep breath. "Oliver Quade, the lunches are on me."

"And the dinner and the show tonight are on me," grinned Oliver Quade.

THE RIDDLE OF THE YELLOW CANARY

BY STUART PALMER

The soft April rain was beating against the windows of Arthur Reese's private office, high above Times Square. Reese himself sat tensely before his desk, studying a sheet of paper still damp from the presses. He had just made the most important decision of his life. He was going to murder the Thorens girl.

For months he had been toying with the idea, as a sort of mental chess problem. Now, when Margie Thorens was making it so necessary that she be quietly removed, he was almost surprised to find that the idle scheme had reached sheer perfection. It was as if he had completed a jig-saw puzzle while thinking of something else.

Beyond his desk was a door. On the glass Reese could read his own name and the word "Private" spelled backwards. As he watched, a shadow blotted out the light, and he heard a soft knock.

"Yes?" he called out.

It was plump, red-haired Miss Kelly—excellent secretary, Kelly, in spite of her platinum finger nails. "Miss Thorens is still waiting to see you," said Kelly.

She had not held her job long enough to realize just how often, and how long, Margie Thorens had been kept waiting.

"Oh Lord!" Reese made his voice properly weary. He looked at his watch, and saw that it was five past five. "Tell her I'm too busy," he began. Then—"No, I'll stop in the reception room and see her for just a moment before I go. Bad news for her again, I'm afraid."

Miss Kelly knew all about would-be song writers. She smiled. "Don't forget your appointment with Mr. Larry Foley at five-thirty. G-night, Mr. Reese.' She closed the door.

Reese resumed his study of the sheet of music. *May Day—a song ballad with words and music by Art Reese, published by Arthur Reese and Company.* He opened the page, found the chorus, and hummed a bar of the catchy music. "I met you on a May day, a wonderful okay day..."

He put the song away safely, and reached into his desk for a large flask of hammered silver. He drank deeply, but not too deeply, and shoved it into his hip pocket.

The outer office was growing suddenly quiet as the song pluggers left their pianos. Vaudeville sister teams, torch-singers, and comics were temporarily giving up the search for something new to interest a fretful and jaded public. Stenographers and clerks were covering their typewriters. The day's work was over for them— and beginning for Reese.

From his pocket he took an almost microscopic capsule. It was colorless, and no larger than a pea. Yet it was potentially more dangerous than a dozen cobras...a dark gift of fortune which had started the whole plot working in his mind.

Three years ago an over-emotional young lady, saddened at the prospect of being tossed aside "like a worn glove," had made a determined effort to end her own life under circumstances which would have been very unpleasant indeed for Arthur Reese. He had luckily been able to take the cyanide of potassium from her in time. She was married and in Europe now. There would be no way of tracing the stuff. It was pure luck.

The capsule was his own idea, a stroke of genius. He rolled it in his fingers, then looked at his watch. It was fifteen minutes past five. The lights of Times Square were beginning to come on, clashing with the lingering dullness of the April daylight. Reese picked up a brown envelope which lay on his desk, crossed to his top-coat, and pocketed a pair of light gloves. Then he stepped out into the brilliantly lighted but deserted outer office.

The first door on his right bore only the figure "1" on the glass. It was unlocked, and he stepped quickly through. It did not matter if anyone saw him, he knew, yet it would be safer if not.

Margie Thorens leaped up from the piano stool—the room was furnished so that it could be used by Reese's staff if necessary, and came toward him. Reese smiled with his mouth, but his eyes stared at her as if he had never seen her before.

There had been a time not so long ago when Arthur Reese had thought this helpless, babyish girl very attractive, with her dark eyes, darker hair, and the sullen mouth. But that time was over and done. He steeled himself to bear her kiss, but he was saved from completing that Judas gesture. She stopped, searching his face.

"Sit down, Margie," he said.

She dropped to the stool. "Sit down yourself," she told him. Her voice was husky. "Or do you have to rush away? Making another trip to Atlantic City this week-end?" Her words dripped with meaning. She played three notes on the black keys.

"Forget your grouch," said Reese. "I've got news."

"You'd better have!" She swung on him. "You've got to do something about me. I'm not going to sit out in the cold. Not with what I've got on you, Lothario."

She had raised her voice, and he didn't want that. "Good news," he said hastily. Her eyes widened a little. "Oh, it's not the Tennessee song. That stuff is passé. But I finally got Larry Foley to listen to *May Day*, and he thinks it's great. Another *Echo in the Valley*, he says. So I'm going to publish it. He's willing to plug it with his band over the air, and he'll make a play to get it in the picture he's going to do in Hollywood. You're a success! You're a song writer at last!"

Margie Thorens looked as though she might fall. "It's all true," he assured her. As a matter of fact it was. Reese had known that it would be easier to tell the truth than invent a lie. And it wouldn't matter afterward. "I'm rushing publication, and there'll be a contract for you in the morning."

She was still dizzy. "You—you're not going to horn in as co-author or anything? Truly, Art?"

"You look dizzy," he said. He pulled out his flask. "How about a drink to celebrate?"

Margie shook her head. "Not on an empty stomach," she pleaded. "I'd like a glass of water though."

The carefully designed plan of Arthur Reese rearranged itself, like a shaken kaleidoscope. He hurried to the water-cooler in the corner, and after a second's pause returned with a conical paper cup nearly full. "This will fix you up," he told her.

Margie drained it at one gulp, and he breathed again. He looked at his watch, and saw that it was five-twenty. The capsule would hold for four to six minutes...

"Better still," he rushed on. "I got an idea for a lyric the other day, and Foley likes it. If you can concoct a good sobby tune to go with it..."

He fumbled at his pockets. "I've lost the notes," he said. "But I can remember the lyric if you'll write it down." He handed her a yellow pencil and the brown envelope which held her rejected manuscript of *Tennessee Sweetheart*. "It begins—Good-bye, good-bye—"

He dictated, very slowly, for what seemed to him an hour. He stole a glance at his watch, and saw that four minutes had elapsed. He found himself improvising, repeating a line...

"You gave me that once," protested Margie. "And the rhymes are bad." She raised her head as if she had suddenly remembered some unspeakable and ancient secret. "Turn on the lights!" she cried. "It's getting—Art! I can't see you!" She groped to her feet. "Art—oh, God, what have you done to me..."

Her voice trailed away, and little bubbles were at her lips. She plunged forward, before he could catch her.

Reese found himself without any particular emotion except gratitude that her little body had not been heavy enough to shake the floor. He left her there, and went swiftly to the door. There was no sign that anyone had been near to hear that last desperate appeal. He congratulated himself on his luck. This sort of thing was far simpler than the books had made him suppose.

He closed the door, and shot the bolt which was designed to insure privacy for the musicians. Then he began swiftly to complete his picture—a picture that was to show to the whole world the inevitable suicide of Margie Thorens.

He first donned his light gloves. It was no effort at all to lift the girl to the wicker settee, although he had to resist a temptation to close the staring dark eyes.

He reached for the tiny gold-washed strap-watch that Margie Thorens wore around her left wrist. Here he struck a momentary snag. Reese had meant to set the hands at five of six, and then smash the thing to set the time of the "suicide," but the crystal had broken when she fell.

The watch was not ticking. He removed one glove, and carefully forced the hands of the little timepiece ahead. The shards of broken glass impeded their movement, but they moved. He put his glove back on.

Reese did not neglect to gather up the fragment or two of glass which had fallen on the oak floor, and place them where they would naturally have been if the watch had been broken against the arm of the settee in her death agony. Luckily the daylight lingered.

The paper cup was on the floor. He was not sure that finger-prints could be wiped from paper, so he crumpled it into his pocket. Taking another from the rack, he sloshed a bit of water into it, and then dropped in a few particles of the poison which he had saved for some such purpose. The mixture he spilled about the dead mouth and face, and let the cup fall where it would have fallen from the nerveless fingers. On second thought, he picked it up, placed it in the limp hand of Margie Thorens, and crumpled it there with his gloved hand.

It was finished—and water-tight, he knew that. Who could doubt that a young and lonely girl, stranded in New York without friends or family, disappointed in her ambitions and low in funds, might be moved to take her own life?

Reese looked at his watch. The hands had barely passed the hour of five-thirty-five. He had twenty minutes to establish a perfect alibi if he should ever need one.

There still remained a ticklish bit of fine work. He unlocked the door and looked out into the main office. It was still deserted. He stepped out, leaving the door ajar, and put his arm inside to turn the brass knob which shot the bolt.

Pressing the large blade of his jack-knife against the spring lock, he withdrew his arm and swung the door shut. Then he pulled away the knife, and the latch clicked. Margie Thorens was dead in a room which had a window without a fire escape, and a door locked on the inside.

In two minutes Reese was laughing with the elevator boy on his way down. In five more he stepped out of the men's room at the Roxy Grill, washed and groomed, and with the paper cup and the folded paper which had held poison and capsule all gone forever via the plumbing. When the big clock above the bar pointed to ten of six, Reese had already stood Larry Foley his second round of drinks. He was softly humming *May Day*.

Inspector Oscar Piper called Spring 7-3100 before he put on his slippers. "Anything doing, Sergeant?"

"Nothing but a lousy suicide of a dame up in Tin Pan Alley," the phone sergeant said. "Scrub woman found her, and the precinct boys are there now."

"I'll stop in and have a look in the morning," decided the Inspector. "These things are all alike."

The morrow was a Saturday, and Miss Hildegarde Withers was thus relieved of the necessity of teaching the young how to sprout down in Jefferson School's third grade. But if she had any ideas of lying abed in luxurious idleness, they were rudely shattered by the buzzing of the telephone.

"Yes, Oscar," she said wearily.

"You've often asked me how the police can spot a suicide from a murder," Piper was saying. "Well, I'm on the scene of a typical suicide, perfect in every detail but one and that doesn't matter. Want to have a look? If you hurry you'll have a chance to see the stiff before she goes to the morgue."

"I'll come," decided the school teacher. "But I shall purposely dawdle in hopes of missing your exhibit."

Dawdle as she did, she still rode up the ten stories in the elevator and entered the offices of Arthur Reese, Music Publisher, before the white-clad men from the morgue arrived. Her long face, somewhat resembling that of a well-bred horse, made a grimace as the Inspector showed her the broken lock of the little reception and music room, and what lay beyond.

"Scrub women came in at midnight, and found the door locked. They got the night watchman to break it, since it couldn't have been locked from outside, and thought somebody was ill inside or something. Somebody was. The medical examiner was out on Long Island over that latest gang killing, and couldn't get here till a couple of hours ago, but he found traces of cyanide on her mouth. The autopsy will confirm it, he says."

Miss Withers nodded. "She looks awfully—young," she said.

"She was," Piper told her. "We've checked up on the kid. Ran away from an Albany high school to make her fortune as a songwriter, so she's even younger than you thought. Been in New York five months and got nothing but rejections. Yesterday afternoon she got another one and she waited until everyone else had gone, and bumped herself off. Left a suicide note on the piano, too." The Inspector handed over the brown envelope. "Wrote it on the envelope which held the bad news—her rejected manuscript. And notice how firm and steady the writing is, right to the last word almost."

Miss Withers noticed. She bent to squint over the rhymed note. She saw:

"Good-bye, good-bye I cry
A long and last good-bye
Good-bye to Broadway and the lights
Good-bye to sad days and lonely nights
I've waited alone
To sing this last song
Good-bye…"

She read it through again. "She didn't sign it," Piper went on. "But it's her handwriting all right. Checks with the manuscript of the rejected song in the envelope, and also with a letter in her handbag that she was going to mail."

"A letter?" Miss Withers handed back the envelope. But the letter was a disappointment. It was a brief note to the Metropolitan Gas Company, promising that a check would be mailed very shortly to take care of the overdue bill, and signed "Margery Thorens."

Miss Withers gave it back. She took the tiny handbag that had been the dead girl's, and studied it for a moment. "She had a miniature fountain pen, I see," said the school teacher. "It writes, too. Wonder why she used a pencil?"

"Well, use it she did, because here it is." Piper handed her the long yellow pencil which had lain on the floor. The school teacher looked at it for a long time.

"The picture is complete," said Piper jovially. "There's only one tiny discrepancy, and that doesn't matter."

Miss Withers wanted to know what it was. "Only this," said the Inspector. "We know the time she died, because she smashed her wrist watch in her death throes. That was five minutes to six. But at that hour it's pretty dark—and this is the first time I ever heard of a suicide going off in the dark. They usually want the comfort of a light."

"Perhaps," said Miss Withers, "perhaps she died earlier, and the watch was wrong? Or it might have run a little after she died?"

The Inspector shook his head. "The watch was too badly smashed to run a tick after she fell," he said. "Main stem broken. And she must have died after dark because there was somebody here in the offices until around five-thirty. I tell you…"

He was interrupted by a sergeant in a baggy blue uniform. "Reese has just come in, Inspector. I told him you said he should wait in his office."

"Right!" Oscar Piper turned to Miss Withers. "Reese is the boss of this joint, and ought to give us a line on the girl. Come along if you like."

Miss Withers liked. She followed him into the outer office and through a door marked "Arthur Reese, Private." The Inspector, as was their usual fiction, introduced her as his stenographer.

Reese burst out, a little breathlessly, with "What a thing to happen—here! I came down as soon as I heard. What a—"

"What a thing to happen anywhere," Miss Withers said under her breath.

"Poor little Margie!" finished the man at the desk.

Piper grew suddenly Inspectorish. "Margie, eh? You knew her quite well then?"

"Of course!" Reese was as open as a book. "She's been hounding the life out of me for months because I have the reputation of sometimes publishing songs by beginners. But what could I do? She had more ambition than ability…"

"You didn't know her personally, then?"

Reese shook his head. "Naturally, I took a friendly interest in her, but anyone in my office will tell you that I never run around with would-be song writers. It would make things too difficult. Somebody is always trying to take advantage of friendship, you know."

"When did you last see the Thorens girl?" Piper cut in.

Reese turned and looked out of the window. "I am very much afraid," he said, "that I was the last person to see her alive. If I had only known..."

"'Get this, Hildegarde!" commanded Piper.

"I am and shall," she came back.

"Several weeks ago," began Reese, "Margie Thorens submitted to me a song called *Tennessee Sweetheart*, in manuscript form. It was her fifth or sixth attempt, but it was lousy—I beg your pardon, a terrible song. Couldn't publish it. Last night she came in, and I gave her the bad news. Made it as easy as I could, but she looked pretty disappointed. I had to rush off and leave her, as I had an appointment for five-thirty with Larry Foley, the radio crooner. So I saw her last in the reception room where she died—it must have been five-thirty or a little earlier."

Miss Withers whispered to the Inspector. "Oh," said he, "how did you know that the Thorens girl died in the reception room?"

"I didn't," admitted Reese calmly. "I guessed it. You haven't got that cop standing guard at the broken door for exercise. Anyway, I was a few minutes later for my date because of the rain, but I met Foley at about twenty to six. He'll testify to that, and fifty others."

Piper nodded. He took a glittering gadget from his pocket. "Can you identify this, Mr. Reese?"

Reese studied the watch. "On first glance, I should say that it was Margie's. But I wouldn't know…"

"You wouldn't know, then, if it was usually on time?"

Reese was thoughtful. "Of course I wouldn't. But Margie was usually on time, if that is anything. I said when she phoned me yesterday morning that I'd see her if she came in at quarter to five, and on the dot she arrived. I was busy, and she had to wait."

The Inspector started to put the watch back into its envelope but Miss Withers held out her hand. She wrinkled her brows above it, as the Inspector put his last question.

"You don't know, then, anything about any private love affairs Miss Thorens might have had?"

"Absolutely not. I don't even know where she lived, or anything except that she came from somewhere upstate— Albany I think it was. One of her attempts at song-writing was titled *Amble to Albany*."

Piper and the music publisher walked slowly out of the office, toward where a wicker basket was being swiftly carried through a broken door by two brawny men in white. Miss Withers lingered behind to study the wrist watch which had been Margie Thorens'. It was a trumpery affair with a square modernistic face. Miss Withers found it hard to tell time by such a watch. She noted that the minute hand pointed to five before the hour, and that the hour hand was in the exactly opposite direction. She put it safely away, and hurried after the Inspector.

With the departure of the mortal remains of Margie

Thorens, the offices of Arthur Reese and Company seemed to perk up a bit. The red-haired Miss Kelly returned to her desk outside Reese's office, wearing a dress which Miss Withers thought cut a bit too low in front for business purposes. The clerks and stenographers were permitted to fill the large room again, somewhere a man began to bang very loudly upon a piano, and an office boy rushed past Miss Withers with a stack of sheet music fresh from the printer's.

"Well, we'll be off," said the Inspector suddenly, in her ear.

Miss Hildegarde Withers jumped. "Eh? Well what?"

"We'll leave. This case is plain as the nose—I mean, plain as day. Nothing here for the Homicide Squad."

"Naturally," said Miss Withers. But her thoughts were somewhere else.

The Inspector had learned to heed her suggestions. "Anything wrong? You haven't found anything that I've missed, have you?"

Hildegarde Withers shook her head. "That's just the trouble," she said. "I'm beginning to suspect myself of senility."

"Tell me," said Miss Withers that evening, "just what are the clues which spell suicide so surely?"

"First, the locked door to insure privacy," said the Inspector. "Second, the suicide note, for it's human nature to leave word behind. Third, the motive—in this case, melancholy. Fourth, the suicide must be an emotional, neurotic person. Get me?"

"Clear as crystal," said Hildegarde Withers. "But granted that a girl chooses to die in darkness, why does she write a suicide note in darkness? And why does she bend a pencil?"

"But the pencil wasn't bent!"

"Exactly!" said Hildegarde Withers, thoughtfully.

To all intents and purposes, that ended the Thorens case. Inspector Oscar Piper turned his attention to weightier matters. Medical Examiner Bloom reported, on completion of the autopsy, that the deceased had met death at her own hands through taking a lethal dose of cyanide of potassium, probably obtained in a college or high school laboratory, or perhaps from a commercial orchard spray.

Miss Hildegarde Withers attended to her usual duties down at Jefferson School, and somewhere in the back of her mind a constant buzzing continued to bother her. The good lady was honestly bewildered by her own stubbornness. It was perfectly possible that the obvious explanation was the true one. For the life of her she could think of no other that fit even some of the known facts. And yet—

On Tuesday, the fourth day after the death of Margie Thorens, Miss Withers telephoned to Inspector Piper, demanding further information. "Ask Max Van Donnen how long the girl could have lived after taking the poison, will you?"

But the old German laboratory expert had not analyzed the remains, said Piper. Dr. Bloom had summarized the findings of the autopsy—and Margie Thorens had died an instant death. In her vital organs was a full grain of cyanide of potassium, one of the quickest known poisons.

"She couldn't have taken the poison and then written the note?" asked Miss Withers.

"Impossible," said the Inspector. "But what in the name of—"

Miss Withers had hung up. Again she had struck a stone wall. But too many stone walls were in themselves proof that something was a little wrong in this whole business.

That afternoon Miss Withers called upon a Mrs. Blenkinsop, the landlady who operated the rooming house in which Margie Thorens had lived. She found that lady fat, dingy, and sympathetic.

"I read in the papers that the poor darling is to be sent home to her aunt in Albany, and that her class is to be let out of high school to be honorary pall-bearers," said Mrs. Blenkinsop. "Such a quiet one she was, the poor child. But it's them that runs deep."

Miss Withers agreed to this. "Do you suppose I could see her rooms?"

"Of course," agreed the landlady. "Everything is just as she left it, because her rent was paid till the end of April, and that's a week yet." She led the way up a flight of stairs. "You know, the strangest thing about the whole business was her going off that way and making no provision for her pets. You'd a thought—"

"Pets?"

The landlady threw open a door. "Yes'm. A fine tortoise shell cat, and a bird. A happy family if ever I saw one. I guess Miss Thorens was lonesome here in the city, and she gave all her love to them. Feed and water 'em I've done ever since I heard the news..." She snapped her fat fingers as they came into a dark, bare room furnished with little more than the bare necessities of life. It was both bedroom and sitting room, with the kitchenette in a closet and a bath across the hall. One large window looked out upon bare rooftops. One glance told Miss Withers that the room existed only for the rented grand piano which stood near the window.

Mrs. Blenkinsop snapped her fingers again, and a rangy, half-grown cat arose from the bed and stretched itself. "Nice Pussy," said Mrs. Blenkinsop.

Pussy refused to be patted, and as soon as she had made sure that neither visitor carried food she returned to her post on the pillow. Both great amber eyes were staring up at the gilt cage which hung above the piano, in the full light of the window. Inside the cage was a small yellow canary, who eyed the intruders balefully and muttered, "Cheep, cheep."

"I've got no instructions about her things, poor darling," said the landlady. "I suppose they'll want me to pack what few clothes she had. If nobody wants Pussy, I'll keep her, for there's mice in the basement. I don't know what to do with the bird, for I hate the dratted things. I got a radio, anyhow…"

The woman ran on interminably. Miss Withers listened carefully, but she soon saw that Mrs. Blenkinsop knew less about Margie Thorens than she did herself. The woman was sure, she insisted, that Margie had never had men callers in her room.

More than anything, Miss Withers wanted a look around, though she knew the police had done a routine job already. She wondered if she must descend to the old dodge of the fainting spell and the request for a glass of water, but she was saved from it by a ring at the bell downstairs.

"I won't be a minute," promised Mrs. Blenkinsop. She hastened out of the door. Miss Withers made a hurried search of bureau drawers, of the little desk, the music on the piano...and found nothing that gave her an inkling. There were reams of music paper, five or six rejected songs in manuscript form...that was the total. The room had no character.

Miss Withers sat down at the piano and struck a chord. If only this instrument, Margie's one outlet in the big city, could speak! There was a secret here somewhere...for the understanding eye and heart to discover. Miss Withers let her fingers ramble over the keys, in the few simple chords she knew. And then the canary burst into song!

"Dickie!" said the school teacher. "You surprise me." All canaries are named Dickie, and none of them know it. The bird sang on, improvising, trilling, swinging gaily by its tiny talons from the bottom of its trapeze. Miss Withers realized that there was a rare singer indeed. Her appreciation was shared by Pussy, who dug shining claws into the cover of the bed and narrowed her amber eyes. The song went on and on...

Miss Withers thought of something. She had once read that the key to a person's character lies in the litter which accumulates beneath the paper in his bureau drawers. She hurried back to the bureau and explored again. She found two dance programs, a stub of pencil, pins, a button, and a smashed cigarette, beneath the lining.

She was about to replace the paper when she heard someone

ascending the stairs. That would be Mrs. Blenkinsop. Hastily she jammed the wearing apparel back in the drawer, and thrust the folded newspaper which had lined it into her handbag. When the door opened she was talking to the still twittering canary.

She took her departure as soon as she could, leaving Mrs. Blenkinsop completely in the dark as to the reasons for her call. "I hope you're not from a tabloid," said the landlady. "I don't want my house to get a bad name…"

Down the street Miss Withers paused to take the bulky folded newspaper from her bag. But she didn't throw it away. It was a feature story clipped from the "scandal sheet" of a Sunday paper—a story which dealt with the secrets behind some of America's song hits, how they were adapted from classics, revamped every ten years and put out under new names, together with photographs of famous song writers.

But the subject of the story was not what attracted Miss Withers' eagle eye. Across the top margin of the paper a rubber stamp had placed the legend— "With the compliments of the Hotel Rex—America's Riviera— Boardwalk."

"Dr. Bloom? This is Hildegarde Withers. Yes, Withers. I have a very delicate question to ask you, doctor. In making your autopsy of the Thorens girl's body, did you happen to notice whether or not she was—er, enceinte? It is very important, doctor, or I wouldn't bother you. If you say yes, it will turn suicide into murder.'

"I say no," said crusty Dr. Bloom. "I did and she wasn't." And that was the highest stone wall of all for Hildegarde Withers.

"Where in heaven's name have you been hiding yourself?" inquired the Inspector when Miss Withers entered his office on Friday of that week after the death of Margie Thorens.

"I've been cutting classes," she said calmly. "A substitute is enduring my troop of hellions, and I'm doing scientific research.'

"Yeah? And in what direction?" The Inspector was in a jovial mood, due to the fact that both his Commissioner and the leading gangster of the city were out of town—not together, but still far enough out of town to insure relative peace and quiet to New York City.

"I'm an expert locksmith," Miss Withers told him. "I've spent three hours learning something about poisons from Max Van Donnen, who has forgotten more than the Medical Examiner ever knew! He says you can't swallow a lethal dose of cyanide without dying before it gets to the stomach—*unless it's in a capsule.*"

"You're not still hopped up about the Thorens suicide?" The Inspector was very amused. "Why that's the clearest, open and shut case…"

"Oscar, did you ever hear of a murder without the ghost of a motive?"

He shook his head. "Doesn't exist," he told her. She nodded slowly. "See you later," she said.

Miss Withers rode uptown on the subway, crossed over to Times Square, and came into the offices of Arthur Reese, Music Publisher.

The red-headed Miss Kelly looked up with a bright smile.

"Mr. Reese is very busy just now," she said. Miss Withers took a chair, and stared around the long office. It was a scene of redoubled activity since her last visit, with vaudevillians, song-pluggers, office boys, and radio artists rushing hither and yon. On the wall opposite her was an enlargement in colors of the cover of the new song, *May Day—by Art Reese*. On every desk and table were stacks of copies of the new song, *May Day*.

"So Mr. Reese is a composer as well as a publisher?" Miss Withers asked conversationally.

Miss Kelly was in a friendly mood. "Oh, yes! You know, he wrote that big hit, *Sunny Jim*, which is how he got started in the music business. Of course, that was before I came here…"

"When was it?" asked Miss Withers.

"Two years ago, at least. But *May Day* is going to be a bigger hit than any of them. It's going to be the sensation of the season. All the crooners want it, and the contracts for records are being signed this week."

Miss Withers nodded. "There's a lot of money in writing a song, isn't there?"

"A hit—oh, yes. Berlin made a quarter of a million out of *Russian Lullaby*." Miss Kelly had to raise her voice, as a dozen pianos in a dozen booths were clashing out lilting, catchy music. A door opened somewhere, and Miss Withers heard a sister team warbling soft, close-harmony…"I met you on a May Day, a wonderful okay day, and that was my hey-hey day…a day I can't forget…"

"It's published the first of May," Miss Kelly went on chattily. "And that's why Mr. Reese is so busy. He's got to go out of town this afternoon, and I'm afraid he won't be able to see you today without an appointment."

"Eh?" Miss Withers started. "Yes, of course. No, he won't I mean…I mean…" She rose suddenly to her feet, humming the lilting music of *May Day*. It was familiar, hauntingly familiar. Of course, she had read of how popular tunes were stolen. And yet—suddenly the mists cleared and she knew. Knew where she had heard those first few bars of music—knew what the meaning of it all must be—knew the answer to the riddle. She turned and walked swiftly from the room.

She rode down in the elevator somehow, and stumbled out of it into the main hall. There she stopped short. She could waste no energy in walking. Every ounce of her strength was needed to think with. The whole puzzle was assembling itself in her mind—all the hundred odd and varied bits flying into place. Everything—

She stood there for a long time, wondering what to do. Should she do anything? Wasn't it better to let well enough alone? Nobody would believe her, not even Oscar Piper. Certainly not Oscar Piper.

She stood there until one o'clock struck, and the hall was filled with luncheon-bound clerks and stenographers. Her head was aching and her hands were icy-cold. There was a glitter in her eyes, and her nostrils were extraordinarily wide.

Miss Withers was about to move on when she stopped, frozen into immobility. She saw the elevator descend, saw the doors

113

open…and out stepped the plump, red-haired Miss Kelly.

She was laughing up into the face of Arthur Reese. Reese was talking softly yet clearly, oblivious of everything except the warm and desirable girl who smiled at him…

Miss Withers pressed closer, and caught one sentence—one only. "You'll be crazy about the American Riviera…" he was promising.

Then they were gone.

Miss Withers had three nickels. She made three phone calls. The first was to Penn Station, the second to Mrs. Blenkinsop, and the third to Spring 7-3100. She asked for Inspector Piper.

"Quick!" she cried. "Oscar, I've got it! The Thorens suicide wasn't—I mean it was murder!"

"Who?" asked Piper sensibly.

"Reese, of course," she snapped. "I want you to arrest him quick…"

"But the locked door?"

Miss Withers said she could duplicate that trick, given a knife and the peculiar type of lock that Reese had installed on his music-reception room.

"But the suicide note?"

Miss Withers gave as her opinion that it was dictated, judging by the spaces between words and the corrections made by the writer.

"But—but, Hildegarde, you can't force a person to take poison!" Miss Withers said you could give them poison under the guise of something more innocent.

"You're still crazy," insisted the Inspector. "Why—"

Miss Withers knew what he was thinking. "The alibi? Well, Oscar, the murder was committed at a time when Reese was still in his office, which explains the daylight. He smashed the girl's watch, and then set the hands ahead. But you didn't have sense enough to know that with the minute hand at five of six, the hour hand cannot naturally be exactly opposite! Particles of glass interfered, and the hands of her watch were at an impossible angle!"

Piper had one last shot in his locker. "But the motive?"

"I can't explain, and the train leaves in twenty minutes!" Miss Withers was a bit hysterical. "She's a nice girl, Oscar, even if she has platinum finger-nails. She mustn't go with him, I tell you. If they get out of the state, it means extradition and God knows what—it'll be too late…"

"Take an aspirin and go to bed," said the Inspector kindly. "You're too wrought up over this. My dear woman…" He got the receiver crashed in his ear.

Mr. Arthur Reese was out to enjoy a pleasant week-end. The first balmy spring weather of the year had come, aptly enough, on the heels of his first happy week in many a month. To have *May Day* showing such excellent signs of becoming a hit upon publication day was almost too much.

He made no mistakes. He did not try to kiss Kelly in the taxi, not even after they had picked up her suitcase and were approaching Penn Station. There would be time enough for that later.

"This trip is partly pleasure as well as business," he said to

Miss Kelly. "We both need a rest after everything that's happened this week—and I want you to play with me a little. Call me Art…"

"Sure," said Kelly. "You can call me Gladys, too. But I like Kelly better." She snuggled a little closer to her employer. "Gee, this is thrilling," she said. "I've never been to Atlantic City even—let alone with a man and adjoining rooms and everything…what my mother would say!"

"Very few people would understand about things like this," said Reese comfortably. "About how a man and a girl can have a little adventure together like this— really modern…"

"If you say so," said Kelly, "it's true. You know I've had a crush on you ever since I came to work for you, Mr. Reese—Art…"

"Sure," he said. "And I'm crazy about you, too." He paused, and his eyes very imperceptibly narrowed. "How old are you, Kelly?"

"Twenty," she said wonderingly. "Why?"

"Nice age, twenty," said Reese, taking a deep breath. "Well, Kelly—here we are."

Reese had a stateroom on the Atlantic City Special, and Kelly was naturally pleased and excited by that. She was greener than he had thought. Well, he owed this to himself, Reese thought. A sort of reward after a hard week. It was a week ago today that—

"What are you thinking of?" asked Kelly. "You look so mad."

"Business," Reese told her. He took a hammered silver flask from his pocket. "How about a stiff one?" She shook her head, and then gave in.

116

He took a longer one, because he needed it even worse than Kelly. Then he took her hungrily in his arms. "I mustn't let him know how green I am," thought Kelly.

The door opened, and they sprang apart.

A middle-aged, fussy school teacher was coming into the stateroom. Both Kelly and Reese thought her vaguely familiar, but the world is full of thinnish elderly spinsters.

"This is a private stateroom," blurted Reese.

"Excuse me," said Hildegarde Withers. When she spoke, they knew who she was.

She neither advanced nor retreated. She had a feeling that she had taken hold of a tiger's tail and couldn't let go.

"Don't go with him," she said to Kelly. "You don't know what you're doing."

Kelly, very naturally, said, "Why don't you mind your own business?"

"I am," said Miss Withers. She shut the door behind her. "This man is a murderer, with blood on his hands..."

Kelly looked at Reese's hands. They had no red upon them, but they were moving convulsively.

'He poisoned Margie Thorens," said Miss Withers conversationally. "He probably will poison you, too, in one way or another."

"She's stark mad," said Arthur Reese nervously. "Stark, staring mad!" He rose to his feet and advanced. "Get out of here," he said. "You don't know what you're saying..."

"Be quiet," Miss Withers told him. "Young lady, are you

going to follow my advice? I tell you that Margie Thorens once took a weekend trip with this man to Atlantic City—America's Riviera—and she's having her high school class as honorary pall-bearers as a result of it."

"Will you go?" cried Reese.

"I will not." There was a lurch of the car as the train got under way. Shouts of "all aboard" rang down the platform. "This man is going to be arrested at the other end of the line—arrested for murdering Margie Thorens by giving her poison and then dictating a suicide note to her as—"

Reese moved rather too quickly for Miss Withers to scream. She had counted on screaming, but his hands caught her throat. They closed, terribly...

The murderer had only one thought, and that was to silence forever that sharp, accusing voice. He was rather well on to succeeding when he heard a clear soprano in his ear. "Stop! Stop hurting her, I tell you!"

He pressed the tighter as the train got really under way. And then Kelly hit him in the face with his own flask. She hit him again.

Reese choked, caught the flask and flung it wildly through the window, and dropped his victim. He was swearing horribly, in a low and expressionless voice. He shoved Kelly aside, stepped over Miss Withers, and tore out into the corridor. The porter was standing there, his sepia face gray-green from the sounds he had heard. Reese threw him aside and trampled on him. He fought his way to the vestibule and found that a blue-clad conductor was just closing up the doors. Reese knocked him down, and leaped for the end of the platform.

One foot plunged into the recess between train and platform, and his hands clawed at the air. He fell sidewise, struck a wooden partition which bounded the platform, and scrambled forward.

He leaped to his feet. He was free! It would take a minute for the train to stop. He whirled and ran back along the platform…

He knocked over a child, kicked a dog savagely because its leash almost tripped him, and flung men and women out of his way. The train was stopping with a hissing of air-brakes. He ran the faster…

He saw his way cleared, except for a smallish middle-aged man in a gray suit who was hurrying down the stairs—a man who blinked stupidly at him. Arthur Reese knocked him aside—and was then very deftly flung forward in a double somersault. Deft hands caught his arm, and raised it to the back of his neck, excruciatingly.

"What's all this?" said Inspector Oscar Piper. "What's your blasted hurry?"

Miss Withers came to life to find a porter splashing water in her face, and red-haired Miss Kelly praying unashamed. The train had stopped. "I'm all right," she said. "But where did he go—he got away!"

They came out on the platform to find the Inspector sitting on his captive. "This was the only train that left any station in twenty minutes," said Piper. "I changed my mind and thought I'd better rally round. Somebody better send for the wagon."

An hour or so later Miss Withers sat in an armchair, surrounded by the grim exhibits which line the walls of the Inspector's office in Center Street. She still felt seedy, but not too seedy to outline her deductions as to the manner in which Reese had committed the "suicide" of Margie Thorens. One by one she checked off the points. "I knew that a girl who had a fountain pen in her handbag wouldn't use a pencil to write something unless it was given to her," she said. "It wasn't her own, because it was too long to fit into the bag, unless it miraculously bent. From then on the truth came slowly but surely…"

"But the motive!" insisted Piper. "We've got to have a motive. I've got Reese detained downstairs, but we can't book him without a motive."

Miss Withers nodded. Then—"Did a woman come down to see you, a Mrs. Blenkinsop?"

The Inspector shook his head. "No—wait a minute. She came and went again. But she left a package for you with the desk lieutenant…"

"Good enough," said Miss Withers. "If you'll call Reese in here I'll produce the motive."

Arthur Reese, strangely enough, came quietly and pleasantly, with a smile on his face. There was an officer on either side, but Piper had them go outside the door.

"I'm sorry, madam," said Reese when he saw Miss Withers. "But I lost my head when you said those terrible things. I didn't know what I was doing. If I'd realized that you were a policewoman…"

"You're under arrest for the murder of Margie Thorens," cut in Piper. "Under the law, you may make a confession but you may not make a plea of guilty to a charge of murder..."

"Guilty? But I'm not guilty! This woman here may have made a lot of wild guesses as to how I might have killed Margie Thorens, but man alive—where's my motive? Just because I made love to her months ago..."

"And took her to Atlantic City—before she was eighteen," cut in Miss Withers. "That gave her a hold over you, for she was under the age of consent. Being an ambitious and precocious little thing, she tried desperately to blackmail you into publishing one of her songs. And then you found that she had accidentally struck a masterpiece of popular jingles—this famous *May Day*. So you took the song, and made it your own property by removing Margie. She wrote *May Day*—not you! That's my motive!"

Reese shook his head. "You haven't got any proof," he said confidently. "Where's one witness? That's all I ask! Just one—"

"Here's the one," said Hildegarde Withers calmly. From behind the desk she took up a paper-wrapped bundle. Stripping the newspapers away, she brought out a gilt cage, in which a small yellow bird blinked and muttered indignantly.

Miss Withers put it on the desk. "This was Margie Thorens' family," she said. "One of her only two companions in the long days and nights she spent, a bewildered little girl, trying to make a name for herself in an adult's world." She clucked to the little bird, and then, as the ruffled feathers subsided, Miss Withers began to whistle. Over and over again she whistled the first bar of the unpublished song hit, *May Day*.

"I met you on a May day..."

"Who-whew whew-whee whee whee," continued Dickie happily, swelling his throat. On through the second, through the third bar...The Inspector gripped the table top.

"Reese, you said yourself that you never called on Miss Thorens and never knew where she lived," said Hildegarde Withers triumphantly. "Then I wish you'd tell me how her canary learned the chorus of your unpublished song hit!"

Arthur Reese started to say something, but there was nothing to say. "I talked to a pet store man this morning," said Miss Withers, "and he said that it's perfectly possible to teach a clever canary any tune, provided he hears it over and over and over. Well, Dickie here is first witness for the prosecution!"

Arthur Reese's shrill hysterical laughter drowned out anything else she might have said. He was dragged away, while the canary still whistled.

"I'm going to keep him," said Miss Withers impulsively. She did keep Dickie, for several months, only giving him away to Mrs. Macfarland, wife of her Principal, when she learned that he would never learn any other tune but *May Day*...

It was December when Inspector Piper received an official communication. "You are invited to attend, as a witness for the State of New York, the execution of Arthur Reese at midnight, January 7th...Sing Sing, Ossining, New York per L. E. I."

"With pleasure," said the Inspector.

SWEATING IT OUT
WITH DOVER

BY JOYCE PORTER

Every English summer, no matter how awful the weather is in general, is blessed with one gloriously hot, really sweltering day—and in drought years we sometimes have two. The savage murder of young Elvin Garlick took place on one of these exceptional days when the sky was blue and the sun blazed down. So, too, did Detective Chief Inspector Wilfred Dover's 'investigation'. Indeed, his conduct of the case and the highly unseasonable weather were not unconnected.

It was getting on for midday when Detective Chief Inspector Dover, chaperoned as always by MacGregor, his young and handsome sergeant, arrived at Skinners Farm. The temperature was already pushing up into the eighties and most people would have been delighted at getting out into the country on such a marvellous day. Chief Inspector Dover, however, wasn't most people and, in spite of appearances, Skinners Farm was only twenty-five miles from Charing Cross and so not really country anyhow.

Charitable people might have thought it was the heat which had addled Dover's brains but, in reality, he was just as slow-witted on even the most temperate day. On this occasion he didn't seem able to get it into his head that

Skinners Farm wasn't actually a farm, but an over-restored Georgian house standing in its own grounds and separated from the hurly-burly of the outside world by a couple of fields full of gently ruminating black and white cows.

'I suppose they call it a farm, sir,' said MacGregor, surreptitiously dabbing at the back of his neck with a slightly starched white handkerchief, 'because it was once the farmhouse.'

'Bloody fools,' said Dover, the sweat standing out in beads on his forehead. As a concession to the weather, he had left off his overcoat—but the greasy bowler hat, the blue serge suit, and the down-at-heel boots were the same as ever. ''Strewth,' panted Dover, 'but it's hot!'

'Perhaps we could have the window down a bit, sir,' said MacGregor, who'd been wondering for some time if the peculiar smell in the police car was Dover or merely something agricultural they were spraying on the fields.

'I hope they've shifted that blooming body,' said Dover querulously as he plucked at his shirt. 'It'll be ponging to high heaven else.'

MacGregor glanced at his watch. 'They may not have moved it yet, sir,' he warned. 'It's only about an hour and a half since they found him, and since I understand he's lying in some sort of copse and reasonably sheltered from the sun—'

'You won't get me going to see it,' declared Dover flatly. 'I'll bet it's all crawling with flies. Here'—he roused himself as the car turned into a driveway—'are we there?'

The married couple who lived at Skinners Farm were, understandably, in a state of some distress and they greeted the arrival of the two high-powered detectives from Scotland Yard as though it was a heaven-sent solution to all the horrors of that terrible morning. Anxiously hospitable, they conducted a profusely sweating Dover through the house and out on to the comparatively cool and shady veranda.

Here they installed him on a cane chaise longue, plied him with cigarettes, and asked him what he would like in the way of a long, cool drink. Dover, having graciously accepted pretty little Mrs Hewson's suggestion of an iced lager, hoisted his boots up on to the footrest and flopped back. 'Strewth, this was the life! And it was going to take more than a bloody murder case to dislodge him from it.

When, a few minutes later, Mr Hewson came out with the drinks, Dover was more or less obliged to open his eyes. Having half a pint of ice-cold liquid sloshing around in his stomach had quite a bracing effect on him, however, and for a few minutes he was actually sitting up and taking some interest in his surroundings. The veranda, he discovered, overlooked a large and well-kept garden which fell gently away from the house. In the distance was what appeared to be a clump of trees where several figures in dark blue could dimly be seen moving about.

Dover had no wish to strain his eyesight by peering through the heat haze, so he treated himself to a good look at his host instead. Mr Hewson, he ascertained without much interest, was a man of about fifty, but very fit and youthful looking. He was wearing a pair of powder-blue shorts and matching T-shirt, but his manner was far from being carefree and relaxed. As he explained with an uneasy laugh, he wasn't accustomed to stumbling over dead bodies in the middle of a Saturday morning.

Dover relieved his own inner tensions with a good belch and wiped the back of his hand across his mouth. 'You found him, did you?'

'No, not exactly,' said Mr Hewson. 'Tansy, here'—he indicated his wife who was happily engaged in refilling Dover's glass—'actually found him, but naturally I went down to have a look before I phoned the police. I hoped,' concluded Mr Hewson with a bleak little smile, 'that she'd got it wrong.'

'Still hanging around, are they?' asked Dover through a yawn which gave everybody a fine view of his dentures.

'The local police? Yes. The Inspector's using the phone in the sitting-room and the rest of them are still down there in the old orchard.' Mr Hewson pointed toward the clump of trees which Dover had already more or less noticed. 'They're searching through the undergrowth. Er—do you want me to tell them you're here?'

The last thing Dover wanted was a mob of local flatfoots swarming all over him in that heat. He leered encouragingly at pretty little Mrs Hewson. 'So what happened, missus?' he asked and rattled his now empty glass.

Pretty little Mrs Hewson grew tearful. She'd told her story four times already and really didn't want to go through it all again.

Dover had little sympathy for a woman who seemed incapable of recognising an empty glass when she saw one. 'Oh, get on with it!' he advised impatiently.

Mrs Hewson gulped, dried her eyes on a wisp of handkerchief, clutched her husband's hand, and complied. 'It's all my fault, actually. If I hadn't decided to grub up the old orchard and turn it into a vegetable garden, none of this would ever have happened. Freddie wasn't a bit keen on the idea—were you, darling? He said he'd do it himself in time but—well, I know how busy he is, so I got hold of this young man from the village to come and do it.'

'What young man?' demanded Dover, sportingly moving his empty glass even nearer so as to give Mrs Hewson every chance.

'The young man who's been murdered. Elvin Garlick. He works for a firm of landscape gardeners so, of course, he's able to borrow their equipment.'

'You mean he was doing the job for you in his own time?' MacGregor, sipping straight lemonade because he didn't drink when he was on duty, was taking notes. Well, somebody in that partnership had to behave responsibly, didn't they?

'Oh, yes!' said Mrs Hewson with some pride. 'And for cash. That way you get it cheaper because nobody has to pay income tax or VAT or anything. The only trouble was,' she added with a disconsolate little moue, 'he could only come on week-ends and that meant I couldn't keep it a secret from Freddie. I'd wanted to present him with a *fait accompli*, you see.'

'Ugh,' grunted Dover, just to show he was still awake.

'Well, Elvin arrived about half-past eight this morning.' Mrs Hewson raised her pretty little chin defensively. 'He told me to call him Elvin. He said everybody always did, especially when he was obliging them. Well, I told him exactly what I wanted doing and left him to get on with it.'

127

'And where were you all this time, sir?' MacGregor turned to Mr Hewson.

'I was still getting up. Saturday's my day off, too, you know.' Freddie Hewson felt that further explanation was required. 'I'm a stockbroker so, of course, I'm in the City all week.'

'So you didn't see Mr Garlick?'

'No. I knew somebody'd come to the house, of course, and then later you could hear his rotivator or whatever churning away down there in the orchard. That's when this naughty little girl here'—Mr Hewson squeezed his wife's hand affectionately—'finally had to tell me what she was up to.'

'He was ever so surprised!' simpered little Mrs Hewson happily.

'And then what, sir?'

'Well, then nothing, Sergeant. Tansy and I had breakfast out here on the veranda. Garlick was all right then because we could hear him—couldn't we, darling? After breakfast I went round to the back of the house to work on my car. I'm rebuilding a 1934 Alvis and there were a few things I wanted to get done before it got too hot.'

'And you, Mrs Hewson?'

'I was in the kitchen, getting as much as I could ready for dinner tonight. Well, you don't want to spend a glorious day like this slaving over a hot stove, do you?'

'The kitchen's on the far side of the house, too, Sergeant,' explained Mr Hewson, 'so neither of us could see anything going on in the old orchard. And, as I told the other police-man, we didn't hear anything, either. We were both pretty absorbed in what we were doing and, of course, Garlick was a good way off and he wasn't using his machinery the whole time. Well, at about eleven, I suppose it would be, Tansy brought me out a cup of coffee to the garage. She said she was going to take some down to Garlick, too. I would have gone myself, of course, but I'd just started stripping down the clutch and it was all a bit fraught and I didn't want to leave it.'

'Oh, I didn't mind, lovie!' cooed Mrs Hewson. 'Like I said, I was glad to get out of that kitchen for a few minutes and stretch my legs.'

MacGregor nodded. 'So you walked down to the old orchard with the coffee, Mrs Hewson?'

'That's right. Well, when I got there, I couldn't see or hear Elvin anywhere, so I shouted his name. I wasn't keen to go tramping about down there because it's waist-high in weeds and nettles and things.' Mrs Hewson stretched out her shapely bare legs for the general delectation and to empha-sise the point she was making.

MacGregor did, indeed, begin to sweat a bit more freely, but it was many moons since any part of the female anatomy had sent the blood racing through Dover's veins. He merely pushed his bowler hat a bit farther back on his head and inquired if anybody'd got a cigarette to spare.

The murder investigation ground to a halt as the Hewsons obligingly rushed off in all directions to fetch cigarettes, matches and ashtrays. They finally redeemed themselves by refilling Dover's glass, and it was only when they'd got Dover happily swilling and sucking away that Mrs Hewson was able to finish her story.

The end proved something of an anticlimax. Having received no answer to her shouts, Mrs Hewson had gingerly ventured farther into the old orchard and found Garlick just lying there, face down, with his own pitchfork sticking out of his back. Pretty little Mrs Hewson wasn't sure whether she'd screamed, but she was certain she hadn't touched the body.

'I didn't have to,' she exclaimed unhappily. 'I just knew he was dead. I dropped everything and came running back up here to tell Freddie.'

Mr Hewson took up the tale. 'I went tearing down to the old orchard,' he said, 'and there he was. I couldn't see any sign of breathing—Garlick was stripped to the waist, by the way— and with that pitchfork pinning him to the ground...well, I knew it couldn't be an accident or anything. I left everything just as it was and came back up here and phoned the police.'

'And we had a patrol car here in less than five minutes.' A man who had been waiting just inside the sitting-room for a suitably dramatic moment stepped forward. There was an unmistakable drop of the jaw when he got his first clear look at Dover, but he recovered well and introduced himself. 'Detective Inspector Threlfall, sir. I arrived at eleven twenty-six in response to an urgent summons from the patrol car and I have been in charge of the preliminary investigation since my arrival.'

Detective Inspector Threlfall paused in case the seventeen and a quarter stone of solid flesh stretched out on the chaise longue wished to make some response. It didn't. With the mercury climbing that high in the thermometers, Dover had no energy to spare for social niceties.

Inspector Threlfall cleared his throat and tried again. 'You'll want to see the body, sir.'

That stung Dover into life. 'I bloody shan't!' he growled, the mere thought of venturing out into that hot bright world outside making him feel quite sick.

'The doctor thought that Garlick had been knocked unconscious with a blow across the back of the head, sir.' Inspector Threlfall would never have believed that Dover didn't care a fig either way. 'Then he was run through with the pitchfork while he was still out. Crude, but effective.'

MacGregor took pity on the Inspector. 'Are there any signs as to which way the murderer came, sir?'

Inspector Threlfall shook his head. 'Not so far, Sergeant. Mind you, Buff had been churning things up for a couple of hours before he bought it, so it's a tricky job trying to sort things out. Mind you, the murderer could have come from almost any direction. Crept down this way past the house or come across those fields or'—Inspector Threlfall waved his arms about in the appropriate directions—'got into the orchard from the other side. You can't see it from here, but there's a road running along there, not fifty yards from where Buff was killed.'

Dover's chair creaked pathetically as he tried to find a more comfortable position.

'Buff?' queried MacGregor with a frown.

Inspector Threlfall shrugged. 'That was his nickname. I've known him since he was old enough to appear before a juvenile court, you know, and he's been a regular customer ever since. We're going to miss him. He'd had a go at pretty well everything—pinching old ladies' pension books, drunk and disorderly, breaking and entering, nicking cars, shoplifting—'

'Good heavens!' gasped Mrs Hewson faintly.

Inspector Threlfall glanced at her with just a touch of contempt. 'That's how he got his job with Wythenshaw's, madam. His probation officer swung it for him. Well, they'd tried everything else. Seems they thought a spell of honest toil might sort him out. I don't know what old Wythenshaw's going to say when he finds out Buff's been "borrowing" all that expensive gear.'

'But he told me his boss was only too willing to lend him the stuff,' protested Mrs Hewson, carefully avoiding her husband's eye.

'Well, he would, wouldn't he, madam?' asked Inspector Threlfall easily. 'Always had a very smooth tongue, young Buff, especially where the ladies were concerned.' He turned back to MacGregor. 'That's where I'd start looking, if I was you, Sergeant. Buff's got more girls into trouble than you and I've had hot dinners. There must be hundreds of fathers and husbands and boyfriends thirsting for his blood—and that's not counting any members of the fair sex who might have had it in for him.'

'It hardly sounds like a woman's crime,' said MacGregor

doubtfully. He was dying to get down to the old orchard and see things for himself.

'I don't see why not. You don't need much strength to knock somebody out with a chunk of wood or something, and that pitchfork had prongs as sharp as a razor. It would go through him like a hot knife through butter.'

'Oh, dear!' moaned Mrs Hewson, clamping both hands across her mouth and going as white as a sheet.

Her husband leapt across, and wrapping his arms protectively round her, helped her to her feet. He smiled apologetically at the three stolidly staring policemen. 'She's a bit upset, I'm afraid. I'll get her to have a little lie-down. You don't want us any more just now, do you? I think we've told you all we know.'

Nobody seemed much concerned one way or the other, though Dover did bestir himself to remark that, if Mr Hewson was thinking of making his wife some tea, he—Dover—wouldn't say no to a cup.

'These cold drinks are all right,' said Dover confidingly to an astonished Inspector Threlfall, 'but there's nothing to touch a good hot cup of tea, especially in this bloody weather. It brings you out in a good muck sweat.'

'Oh—quite,' said Inspector Threlfall. 'Er—I was wondering what your plans were, sir.'

'Plans?' Dover squinted suspiciously.

'I thought you might like to pop down to the village, sir, and have a word with the lad's mother. He lived with her and she might just know something. I've got some chaps out making general enquiries around the neighbourhood, but I thought I'd best leave Mrs Garlick for you.'

There was an awkward pause. Not that Dover was hesitating. Wild horses weren't going to shift him off that veranda until the temperature outside dropped by at least twenty degrees, but there was the problem of conveying this message to Inspector What's-his-name without too much loss of face. 'How many people knew he was going to be working here this morning?' asked Dover in an attempt to give himself time to think.

Inspector Threlfall rubbed his chin. 'Not many, I should think. Not if he was borrowing the gear without permission. Besides, it's not the sort of thing you'd expect young Buff to be doing in his spare time. Normally, if he wanted extra money, he'd just nick it.'

MacGregor wiped the perspiration off his upper lip. The veranda was only comparatively cool. 'Maybe he's turned over a new leaf?'

'More likely casing the joint,' said Inspector Threlfall. 'The Hewsons must have been mad to let him come within a mile of this place.'

MacGregor fanned himself gently with his notebook. 'It was more Mrs Hewson, wasn't it? I don't think her husband knew anything about it until Garlick turned up this morning.'

'Seems he wanted that old orchard left just as it was,' said Inspector Threlfall. 'Claims it's a nature reserve or something. I reckon he'll pin her ears back for her when all this is over.'

Most untypically at this stage in the proceedings, Dover

was wide awake and listening intently. It wasn't, however, the lethargic conversation about the Hewsons' private life that was claiming his anxious attention, but the more interesting rumbles that were coming from his stomach.

MacGregor laughed a cool, sophisticated, man-of-the-world laugh. 'Hewson'll just have to teach her who's boss, otherwise he won't be able to call his soul his own.'

'Hark who's talking!' jeered Dover, for whom it was never too hot and sticky to be unpleasant. He left his guts to take care of themselves for a moment. 'You could write all you know about married life on a threepenny bit, laddie, and still have room for the Lord's Prayer. Any moron can see that she's got him by the short and curly. What do you expect when a man goes and marries a flighty young thing half his age?'

'I don't think he's quite as—'

'Near as damn it!' snarled Dover, who didn't care to be contradicted, especially when he wasn't feeling too frisky in the first place. 'There's no fool like an old fool.'

'Speaking of marriage,' said Inspector Threlfall—but nobody was listening to him.

Dover had tuned in to those ominous visceral splutterings again and MacGregor was frantically trying to work out if Dover had spotted something he'd missed.

'Do you think it might be a case of jealousy, sir?' MacGregor asked, eyeing Dover doubtfully.

Dover blinked. 'Eh?'

MacGregor grew even more worried. 'The elderly husband, sir, and the attractive young wife? Plus the sexy young man from the village? Do you think there could have been anything between Mrs Hewson and Garlick?' MacGregor appealed to Inspector Threlfall. 'You did say Garlick was attractive to women, didn't you, sir?'

'Like a honeypot to flies,' agreed Inspector Threlfall.

'Or, maybe'—MacGregor was more interested in his own brilliant deductions—'it was *Mrs* Hewson! She takes the coffee down to the old orchard, say, and Garlick makes improper advances towards her. She repulses him. He persists. She picks up the nearest fallen branch or what-have-you and—'

'Bunkum!' said Dover, coming out in a hot flush at the mere thought of such an expenditure of energy in that heat. 'She'd not have the strength. She's only knee-high to a grasshopper.'

'Garlick wasn't all that big a chap, sir,' said Inspector Threlfall as he remembered that these two Scotland Yard experts hadn't yet even seen the body. 'A woman might have done it. But what I wanted to mention, sir, was about the Hewsons.'

'Well, why don't you spit it out, then? I haven't got all bloody day to sit around waiting for you to come to the point.'

The training that Inspector Threlfall had received at the police school all those years ago stood him in good stead now. Otherwise Skinners Farm might have witnessed another and even bloodier murder. 'They're not actually husband and wife, sir. Not legally, that is.'

Dover shrugged his ample shoulders and folded his hands over his ample paunch. 'So what? It's no skin off my nose.' He closed his eyes against the glare coming in from the garden, only to snap them open again as the desire to score off a brother police officer proved stronger than the longing for a quiet forty winks. 'She wears a wedding ring,' he pointed out, much to MacGregor's amazement because one didn't really expect Dover to notice such things. 'And she calls herself "Mrs".'

'That's as maybe, sir,' said Inspector Threlfall, nobly swallowing the rejoinder he would have liked to have made. 'But they are definitely not married—well, not to each other. Hewson's already got a wife. Or as far as anybody knows, he has.'

'And what the hell's that supposed to mean?'

'It's just that I happened to be involved when she did a bunk, sir. The first Mrs Hewson, that is. I was on duty when Hewson came in to report that she was missing. It must be six years ago now. He wanted us to find her.'

'But you didn't?'

'There's nothing we can do about a runaway wife, sir. You know that. I carried out a routine investigation but there was nothing suspicious about her disappearance. All I could do was suggest to Mr Hewson that he try the Salvation Army, not that it was her sort of thing, really.'

Working on the principle that 'talk, talk on the veranda' was a damned sight better than 'walk, walk across that dirty great garden', Dover demanded more details about the first Mrs Hewson and her mysterious disappearance. Inspector Threlfall was obliged to search his memory. As far as he was concerned, the whole incident had been totally unremarkable. It was true that the first Mrs Hewson had cleared out without a word and nobody had heard from her since, but this could be attributed to pure spite.

'Spite?' queried Dover, almost as though he was interested.

'It makes it difficult for Hewson to divorce her, sir. As things stand now, he's got to wait all of seven years and then apply to the courts for permission to presume that she's dead. Meantime, his hands are tied. You can't serve divorce papers on a woman you can't find. Hewson, himself, reckoned that she'd stay out of sight until the seven years was nearly up and then put in an appearance again, just to be bloody-minded. The marriage was pretty well on the rocks when she left home but she seems to have made up her mind not to let him go without a struggle.'

'You're sure there were no signs of foul play?'

'Quite sure, sir. She'd taken all her clothes and jewellery and her passport. There were a couple of suitcases missing and she'd cleared out their joint banking account. Her car turned up a few weeks later. It had been abandoned in the long-stay car park at Gatwick airport but there were no clues in it as to where she'd gone.'

Dover ran a stubby finger round inside his shirt collar. 'Strewth, it was hot! He hoped What's-his-name wasn't going to be all bloody day with that cup of tea. 'Was there another man?'

'Hewson thought there might be, sir, but he didn't know. She was on her own here quite a bit while he was off working in the City.'

'What about her friends?' Dover might not have been the world's most brilliant detective but, in his long years in the police, even he'd managed to pick up a few bits of technique. 'Did she mention to any of them she was thinking of running away?'

Inspector Threlfall shook his head. 'As far as I can remember, sir, she didn't have any friends. At least, not round here.'

'Relations?' Dover had begun thrashing about in his chair like a stranded porpoise.

Inspector Threlfall watched these antics nervously. Was Fatty having some kind of heatstroke or was he merely trying to hoist himself to his feet? 'Only a sister in Ireland, sir, and they hadn't spoken for years.'

With a final wheeze Dover managed to stand up. Too hot to move, it may have been, but, when Nature calls, even the least fastidious of us is obliged to go. Especially if we have bladders as weak as Dover's. 'Bloody foreign muck!' he grumbled. 'It goes straight through you. I don't know why people can't give you proper English beer.' He turned to MacGregor who was trying to pretend that none of this had anything to do with him. 'Where is it, laddie?'

Long association with Dover had taught MacGregor to give a high priority on every occasion to locating where 'it' was. 'I believe there's a cloakroom at the foot of the stairs, sir.'

Dover departed at an urgent trot, leaving a thoughtful silence behind him on the veranda.

Inspector Threlfall loosened his tie. 'He's a bit of a lad, eh?' he said at last.

MacGregor responded with a thin humourless smile and changed the subject. 'Have you any ideas about who killed Garlick, sir?'

'Some,' said Inspector Threlfall, seeing no particular reason to be helpful. Left alone he reckoned he could have solved this case in a couple of hours flat.

'One of his fellow yobboes, sir?'

'Could be.'

'Friday is usually payday,' observed MacGregor carefully. 'Garlick was a bit of a drinker, I think you said?'

'He liked his pint.'

MacGregor closed his notebook to show that this was an off-the-record conversation. 'You often get drunken rows blowing up on a Friday night. Maybe this one didn't get settled until Saturday morning. I mean, who else—except his mates—would have known he'd be working out here this morning? Apart from Mrs Hewson, that is. He'd have hardly spread the news around, would he? And it would only be a local chap who'd know there was easy access to that old orchard from the road.'

Inspector Threlfall contented himself with raising his eyebrows in an enigmatic sort of way. If that was how the clever dicks from the Yard saw it, good luck to 'em! Inspector Threlfall wasn't going to stick his neck out just to show them where they'd gone wrong.

It seemed a very long time before Dover came waddling back. MacGregor tried to get him to continue on down to the scene of the crime while he was still on his feet, but Dover brushed his sergeant's efforts to one side and flopped back into his chair.

'I've just been out round the back,' he announced.

MacGregor's heart sank. Oh, it was all so mortifying! 'But, sir,' he wailed, 'I told you exactly where the cloakroom was!'

Dover flapped an impatient hand. 'Not that, you fool!' he growled. 'I went there first. It was after when I went round

the back of the house to have a look. Bloody good thing I
did too. Do you know what? You can't see the kitchen from
the garage and you can't see the garage from the kitchen.'

'Sir?'

'That means he did it, laddie!' explained Dover helpfully.
He nodded cheerfully at Inspector Threlfall. 'All we need
now is a bulldozer and a warrant.'

'I beg your pardon, sir?'

Dover's good humour began to evaporate. If there was one
thing that really got to him, it was stupidity, especially on a
blooming hot day like this. 'You got cloth ears or something?'
he asked Inspector Threlfall savagely. 'I've solved your murder
for you. 'Strewth, some people want it with bloody jam on!'

Inspector Threlfall very sensibly clung on to the one bit of
this he could understand. 'You've solved the case, sir?'

'It came to me out there,' said Dover, not without a touch
of pride. 'I wasn't just twiddling my thumbs, you know. Then
I went round the back and Bob's your uncle. It all fits. All you've
got to do is dig up the evidence and charge him with murder.'

'But charge—er—who, sir?'

'Well, What's-his-name, you bloody fool!' roared Dover.
'Who else, for God's sake? Look, this morning he waits until
his wife—or whatever she is—is safely shut up in the kitchen.
Right? Then he nips out of the garage round the *other* side of
the house—get it?—and down across the bloody garden.'

The gesticulations which accompanied this vivid account
were a little uncertain as Dover had not actually seen the ter-
rain he was describing. 'He sneaks into this orchard place, finds

young Who's-your-father, picks up the nearest blunt instrument, and knocks him out. OK? After that, all he has to do is finish the job off with the pitchfork. Easy as shelling peas.'

Rightly deducing that nothing useful was going to emerge from Inspector Threlfall's feebly gaping mouth, MacGregor himself tried to introduce a note of sanity into the proceedings.

'Are you saying that Mr Hewson murdered Garlick, sir? But why should he? He didn't even know Garlick. In fact'—MacGregor riffled officiously through his notebook—'he claims that he'd never even seen Garlick until after he was dead. That's a very definite statement, sir, and easy enough to check.'

Dover scowled. Trust MacGregor to start nit-picking! 'He didn't have to know Garlick,' he said sullenly. 'He'd have croaked anybody.'

'You mean Mr Hewson is some sort of homicidal maniac, sir?'

Dover's scowl blackened. If it hadn't been for the excessively hot weather and MacGregor being such a big strapping chap, Dover might have been sorely tempted to go across and belt him one. Insolent young pup!

'Hewson,' he snarled through gritted dentures, 'would gave killed *anybody* who started digging that old orchard up.'

The penny dropped and MacGregor could have kicked himself. 'You mean—'

'I mean that's where he buried his first blooming wife!' snapped Dover, making sure that MacGregor didn't steal his thunder this time. 'She didn't run away. He killed her and then buried her with all her clothes and jewellery and stuff out there in that orchard.'

Inspector Threlfall recovered his powers of speech. 'But I investigated the first Mrs Hewson's disappearance, sir, and there were no suspicious circumstances.'

''Strewth,' sneered Dover happily, 'you wouldn't know a suspicious circumstance if it jumped up and bit you! Hewson was just too clever for you, that's all.'

'Well, it's true the marriage wasn't a very happy one,' said Inspector Threlfall, meekly accepting the slur on his professional competence, 'but we took that as a motive for her leaving him.' He glanced across at MacGregor for support. 'I suppose we could have Hewson in again and ask him a few questions.'

Dover reacted to this suggestion with unusual passion. 'Not yet, you bloody don't!' he spluttered indignantly. 'I'm still waiting for that cup of tea he promised me!' This must have sounded a bit thin even to Dover's ears. 'Besides,' he added in an attempt to place his policy of inaction beyond all question, 'I've been invited to lunch.

'Look, why don't you two just push off and get that orchard dug up? It'll probably take you two or three hours. Soon as you find the wife's dead body, you can come and tell me. But not before two o'clock at the earliest, mind! Then we can confront What's-his-name with the facts and get a confession out of him. There's nothing to worry about. He's not the stuff heroes are made of. He'll soon co-operate if we shove him around a bit. And now'—the Dover eyelids drooped slowly over the Dover eyes—'why don't you just bug off and leave me to have a quiet think?'

Acknowledgments

The publishers are grateful for permission to include the following copyright material in this anthology:

"The Blue Geranium" from *The Thirteen Problems* by Agatha Christie, copyright Agatha Christie Mallowan 1932; "The Riddle of the Yellow Canary" by Stuart Palmer, copyright © 1934 by Stuart Palmer. Reprinted by permission of John Hawkins and Associates, Inc.; "Sweating It Out with Dover" by Joyce Porter, reproduced with the permission of Curtis Brown Group Ltd, London, on behalf of the Reverend Canon J. R. Porter, copyright © 1980 by Joyce Porter.

While every effort has been made to contact the copyright holders of material used in this collection, in the case of any accidental infringement, concerned parties are asked to contact the publishers.